Happiness

The

John

Simmons

Short

Fiction

Award

University of

Iowa Press

Iowa City

*Ann
Harleman*

Happiness

University of Iowa Press, Iowa City 52242

Library of Congress Cataloging-in-Publication Data

Harleman, Ann.

Happiness / Ann Harleman.

p.   cm.—(The John Simmons short fiction award)

ISBN 0-87745-440-X

I. Title.   II. Series.

PS3558.A624246H36   1994

813'.54—dc20   93-11431

                                                      CIP

98   97   96   95   94   C   5   4   3   2   1

For Bruce, for Sarah

If the world were only pain and logic,

who would

want it?

—MARY OLIVER

Contents

ACKNOWLEDGMENTS

I would like to thank Don Berger, David Black,
    Staige Blackford, Barbara Feldman, John
    Hawkes, Leslie Lawrence, Sally Mack, Harriet
    Ritvo, Bruce Rosenberg, Meredith Steinbach,
    Dabney Stuart, Keith Waldrop, Debra Zussman,
    the Harvard Public Library, the Huntington
    Library, and the Providence Area Writers Group
    (PAW). I thank especially Gail Donovan and
    Elizabeth Searle, and Ilona Karmel, who gave
    me her counsel and her fireproof box.
I am grateful to the Guggenheim Foundation and
    the Rhode Island State Council on the Arts for
    their support.
These stories, in somewhat different form, have
    appeared elsewhere: "Eve and Adam, 1963" in
    the *Nebraska Review*; "In Damascus" in
    Shenandoah; "Happiness" in the *Virginia
    Quarterly Review*; "Urban Fishing" in *Oxford
    Magazine*; "Dancing Fish" in *American Fiction*;
    "Salvage" in the *Greensboro Review*;
    "Someone Else" in the *Chicago Tribune* (1987
    Nelson Algren Awards); "It Was Humdrum" in
    Toyon (1986 Raymond Carver Award); "The
    White Hope of Cleveland" in *Crosscurrents:
    New Work by Award Winners II*; "Imagined
    Colors" (as "Life Class") in the *Madison Review*
    (1989 Chris O'Malley Prize); "Nothing" (as
    part of "The Female Lives in the Body") in the
    Madison Review and broadcast on "The Sound
    of Writing" (1991 PEN Syndicated Fiction
    Award); "The Cost of Anything" in the
    Greensboro Review.

Happiness

In Damascus

―――――

Mrs. Mulholland sat under the catalpa tree in her pale straw hat, in a double layer of shade, watching her daughter Vic's eyes. Vic's glance seemed to pick up each one at the table in turn and stitch them together—Mrs. Mulholland's granddaughter, Jane, her older daughter, Alex, Mrs. Mulholland herself—three generations in some intricate, unreadable pattern, embroidered by the shade of the trees that sheltered one corner of the museum terrace.

Victoria, Alexandra. Mrs. Mulholland had given her daughters spacious, queenly names, perhaps in reaction to her own name, Nan, so heavy and square, like a pair of sensible shoes. But her daughters had remodeled their names to suit the people they'd become; and Alex, closing the circle, had named her own daughter Jane. Once, Nan

Mulholland had thought that she herself might eventually, grown old, shrink to fit her name. It hadn't happened yet, at sixty-eight, and eight years a widow. Leaning back in her cushioned metal chair, in her unseasonable white gauze dress—flecked now with grit from the city on the other other side of the shrubbery, held off by iron palings like a beast at the zoo—she looked neither old nor sick. Though her hair was white now, her skin, suffused with a heart patient's rosiness, was still as fine as lawn, her eyes still that startling blue. Her son-in-law had remarked more than once that it was too bad Alex and Vic took after their father—Tod's brown hair, brown eyes, thick pale skin. Only Vic's long hair was bushy and wild, particularly when, as now, she left it unconfined, whereas Alex had the sleek oval head of an otter.

At the empty chair across from Alex, Vic's glance hesitated before moving on, forcing Mrs. Mulholland to count the additions and sub-tractions since earlier Sundays: Tod, her husband, gone; George, Alexandra's husband, added (or would be if, for once, he got away from the hospital in time); and Jane. Mrs. Mulholland allowed her own gaze to rest on her granddaughter in delight. Jane sat, absorbed, folding her paper napkin into an origami rabbit. Her pale caramel-colored hair was caught tightly on top of her head in a rubber band decorated with blue plastic flowers. Her bare forehead shone, giving her a prim, anxious look.

The plan had been to walk around the museum, a Venetian palazzo implausibly set in the middle of Detroit (Was it, then, the palazzo, the same place? So transplanted, was it a place at all?), and after-wards have lunch. But Jane was hungry; and so here they were on the terrace, which at this early hour they had almost to themselves. One other table, in the opposite corner next to the palazzo entrance, was occupied by two languidly beautiful young men in bright-colored turtlenecks, who looked as if they'd been lacquered. Traffic sounds on a Sunday morning were fewer but more noticeable, each passing car whistling individually through the dense laurel and rhododendron.

In any case, the hour was of no importance, nor the small distrac-tions of the setting. Mrs. Mulholland had an agenda. Revelation was what she had in mind—revelation and, with it, a place of re-entry, a way back into the past. Age had shown her that no matter how much she forgot, she would not be able to forgive herself. If she could tell Alex and Vic about Jack—if they could talk about that time, the three of them together—that, Mrs. Mulholland felt, would be absolution of a sort: as close as she could come to it, at any rate. There was no one else left now to forgive her.

As if to help her, the air on the terrace, warm as tea, was clotted with the scent of some old-fashioned shrub whose name Mrs. Mulholland couldn't remember. Laburnum? It was not quite, but almost, the smell of apricot blossoms heavy on the spring air in Syria, when Tod was First Secretary at the embassy. Across a gap of thirty years, the fragrance put her on the stone pavement of Suleiman's *tarifa* with Jack the last time they were together, when they met to say goodbye, looking out at the wide, shallow pool that reflected the minarets on the monks' quarters one after another, as delicately insistent as a pattern woven in damask. Suddenly Mrs. Mulholland remembered clearly the way Jack used to touch her breasts, polishing the nipples with his palms until the tips were hard and round as agates; and his face above her, growing younger and younger with passion until it melted into the face of a boy.

And now the waiter, coming to take their order, looked amazingly like Kahlil—the eyes, the dark skin stretched sharply over the triangular mask of his face. "Do you want to wait for George?" she asked Alex, who shook her head. "All right. You go first," said Mrs. Mulholland to Vic.

Leaving with their order, the young man dropped his pencil and stooped awkwardly to retrieve it. Mrs. Mulholland contemplated the shiny green seat of his trousers. Though he'd run the house in Damascus well enough and kept the other servants more or less honest, she'd never liked Kahlil. Those flat, obsidian eyes, how they looked at her, how they followed Jack when he came to family gatherings. Kahlil *knew*. The hairs would rise on her bare arms when he came near; and because she was afraid, she did nothing.

"You know," said Vic, "for some reason, this makes me think of— where was it we lived when I was five? We used to have breakfast outdoors at a stone table. A man used to come, some friend of Daddy's, very tall and thin, and tickle the *amah* and make her shriek."

"Oh," said Alexandra with a little breath like a sigh. "I remember. That was in Damascus." Her lips stayed parted; her wet lower lip gleamed. "I was at the convent school then. Kahlil used to take me back and forth every day in the car."

Mrs. Mulholland could remember her struggling with reader and workbook, precise and vigilant: the oldest. That was when she'd first begun to have, very faintly, the vertical line that cut between her brows. Unlike Vic, she had always done all the right things. Vic skated on the surface of every day, the gregarious, ingratiating younger child (Mrs. Mulholland believed in the determining force of birth order as deeply as another woman might believe in astrology), already, regrettably, a saleswoman even then. There would have been those in Damascus, in or out of the Foreign Service, who knew about Jack; it was that kind of place. And Tod had known, though they never spoke about it. But not Alex; not Vic. Mrs. Mulholland looked up through the heart-shaped leaves of the catalpa, its foot-long candles hanging down.

Vic turned to Jane, who sat beside her. "How's kindergarten?"

"Fine. We played 'See the Lion.' It's African. Want to know how it goes?"

"Yes," said Vic and Mrs. Mulholland at the same time.

"Well. First everybody sits in a circle and closes their eyes. Then the teacher goes around behind everybody and taps them on the back. She goes all around the circle. And *one* person—when she taps them, she tags them with this sticky paper, you know? That says LION on it."

"Uh-*huh*," said Vic.

Alex leaned over to straighten the collar of Jane's blue-and-white plaid dress. Jane twisted away from her mother's hand. "Then the teacher yells, LION'S LOOSE! And everybody just walks around normal, and you try to make other people think they're the Lion, when they're not. So they'll roar LION! And get exterminated from the game."

"That does sound like fun," said Mrs. Mulholland.

"I don't get it," said Vic. "Wouldn't you know you weren't the lion as soon as you saw the real lion's back?"

Jane frowned. Alex said, "I'll explain it, honey." She turned to Vic. "The object is to keep the real Lion from figuring out she's the Lion, while you fool other people into thinking they are. If the *real* Lion roars, the game's over. The point is, you have to figure out your place in the game by watching other people's responses to you. That's all you have to go on, and yet you can't trust it."

Vic rolled her eyes at Mrs. Mulholland, who, pretending not to understand, looked blandly back.

"When I was your age," Vic said to Jane, "I used to go to the bazaar, in Damascus. The *souk.*"

"What's that?"

"The *souk?* It's a big outdoor market that has everything you can imagine. Rubies and sapphires in piles that you can run your fingers through. Pineapples and licorice and little cakes covered with sesame seeds. Animals—monkeys and parrots and bears."

This was a lie. Damascus, in Vic's memory, was only flashes: tile floors cool and lumpy under her bare feet, a heavy pink light that lay over everything. Mostly she remembered the convent school, so hard to fit into, the dark hot uniforms that pinched and scratched.

All the same, Jane's pale brows rose even further, and her eyes, the same deep, speaking, bachelor-button blue as her grandmother's, fixed on Vic's face.

"Even," Vic leaned forward, "even—a snake-charmer."

"Oh," breathed Jane. "I *love* snakes. A snake can eat something four times as big as its head."

"Why would it want to?" asked Mrs. Mulholland.

"*Grandma.* That way, it only has to eat once a year."

Alex, smoothing her already smooth hair, straightening her already straight pleats, looked around impatiently for their waiter. "You'd think they could be faster when there're so few people eating."

"It will be along soon, dear," said Mrs. Mulholland.

"Sooner than George, that's for sure," Vic said. It would have been ridiculous to suppose that she, with a career tobogganing along the fast track (second-youngest chief buyer in the history of Marshall Field), a condominium, a boyish married lover, envied her sister. No, indeed: she pitied Alex, who seemed unable to manage her life or the people in it, who had not learned to be either pitiful or imperious enough.

Mrs. Mulholland turned to Alex. "So you're happy with the way the new place is turning out," she said. It was not quite a question.

"Well, it's . . . I don't know. It's fine." In the spring Alex and George had bought a house out in Windsor, large, very elegant; sometimes Alex spent the whole day in her chair in the sunroom, looking out across the garden with her hands folded in her lap, waiting.

"What's the matter?"

"It's those magazines she reads," said Vic. "*Country Life. Suburban Elegance.* Why don't you try subscribing to *Urban Squalor?*"

Ignoring her, Alex said to Mrs. Mulholland, "It's hard to get used to a new place." She hesitated. "It just feels *wrong*—you know?"

"Place is a funny thing," said Mrs. Mulholland. "In the Foreign Service, when we had to move so much— You go through stages in a new place. First you look on from the outside. Then you're sort of a minor character. And then, one day, you're on the inside looking out. Damascus was—"

"Let's not, Mother, please. We've had enough about Damascus. Where *is* that waiter?"

How much, Alex wondered, did she really remember from that time; how much did she dream or reconstruct? Nap time: muted sounds from across the hall, waking in the heavy afternoon light with the taste of sleep sour in her mouth. Jack, that was the man's name. At first she had simply absorbed the knowledge of some intense connection between her mother and the man who visited so often—less than knowledge, really, since it was never a fact that existed separately from her, that she looked at and weighed. Never, until the afternoon she woke to see Kahlil standing in the doorway with his dark eyes on her. His face was blank; yet it was as if he summoned her. When she went out into the corridor, her mother's door was open. She stood silently on the threshold watching the man Jack and her mother, until the blood banged so loud in her ears that she had to turn and run. From that day on, she'd seen their life for what it was: the family as constructed by her mother, arranged like an old-fashioned photograph with everyone in place, frozen in a crazy attempt to look natural— smile, pause, explosion of powder and flash.

Just as Alex rose from her chair to go and look for him, their waiter appeared with a heavy tray that wobbled alarmingly as he set it down. With clumsy, unsure motions, he distributed the food. After he left, Alex traded plates with Vic, baconburger for quiche. Jane seized her tuna-fish sandwich in both hands.

Mrs. Mulholland cut her omelet into small, then smaller, pieces. In the silence, choked syllables from the mourning doves in the trees overhead mingled with the clink of kitchen sounds, the growl and bleat of traffic from the street. Back then, she thought, my heart was too small; now it is too large. When Tod was transferred and they left Damascus, she'd let go of Jack like a stone thrown into the deepest part of the Barada. Probably he'd been dead for years.

There was no one, now, to understand how it was then, in Damascus. The oldest city in the world, so it called itself: an ancient, timeless place. Seasons slipping by almost indistinguishable from each other— the heat of winter; the fiercer heat of summer—marked off by the scent of apricot blossoms, the gleam of fruit among the dark shiny leaves. There was snow on the Golan Heights; but of course she never went there. The world was shut out by the charmed ring of green growth that constant irrigation created. Coaxed across the land, the branches and tendrils of the Barada River became canals, baths, pools, fountains—a vast veiny network turning the city into something it was not. It flowered lush and green out of the bare rock face where the mountains leveled out to join the desert.

No one else left, now, to understand how, in that place of contradiction and ambiguity, that world of veiled talk and veiled women, the Foreign Service wives—those who could not decide to be miserable and call it virtue—found ways to fill the emptiness. They drank; they gambled, shuffling cards and gossiping through the long still afternoons; they took drugs; they took lovers. The afternoon silence spread and trickled everywhere, like the Barada. Who could understand how waiting gave Mrs. Mulholland's life shape? Waiting for Jack to call, to come—not missing him, just waiting. Never knowing when she would see him, she could spend the slow mornings waiting, while her blood bubbled lighter than champagne and her skin swarmed with longing.

No one else, now, to remember how the morning would climb from sheer, rivery coolness to yellow heat; and he would come. The set of his narrow shoulders when he took off his shirt made him seem somehow fragile, evoked in her a tenderness till then reserved for her children. His eyes were dark blue, almost black, opaque as stones. They were set very far apart. When he looked down at her, the pale skin underneath them gathered into narrow folds. "I love this," he muttered. Afterwards they lay side by side, his arm across her belly. The bell for afternoon prayer rang insistently in the heat, and the sun through wooden blinds painted their bodies with light. He looked at her from those shallow-set eyes without turning his head, like a deer.

Taking a breath, then another, Mrs. Mulholland began again. "In Damascus—"

"No," said Alex.

"What's the matter with you? Let Mama talk," Vic said.

Jane looked up. "What?" she said. "Is it a story?"

"I won't have it." Alex, whose emotional metabolism quickly and efficiently converted any feeling into anger, stood up. Her metal chair made a violent sound on the flagstones. She said in a low, fierce voice to Mrs. Mulholland, "I have to live inside my life, and you have to live inside yours. That's the way it is."

The waiter, materializing with a tray full of wineglasses they hadn't ordered, stood uncertainly between Vic and Jane. Vic stood up, too. She was combing her fingers over and over through her wild hair. "Remember Mama's heart."

They were all standing now, all except Jane, who sat looking from one adult face to the next: mother, grandmother, aunt. An anxious line appeared between her brows. Carefully she set the last of her sandwich in the center of her plate.

Forgiveness, Mrs. Mulholland thought; and the word expanded in her mind, ballooning, pressing against the inside of her skull. "Alex," she said. "Can't—"

Alex played her trump card. "*Pas devant les enfants*," she said, as had been said so often, so pretentiously, in her childhood; but shouting now. Her face was red and her hair stuck out in wisps around it. "*Pas devant les enfants!*"

As Mrs. Mulholland began to sink back into her chair—began to think, chastened, of course, what was I thinking of, only myself, as usual—Jane jumped up. She stretched out her arms to her mother. The waiter, standing beside her, wasn't quick enough. Jane's shoulder thumped the bottom of his tray.

Mrs. Mulholland, shuddering from the sudden cool wetness, looked down to see wine splashed in streamers across her white skirt, a rusty reddish color. Wine pooled around her feet, and light through the leaves overhead struck shards of glass. The surface of the day shivered.

"God, I'm sorry, Mother," said Alex. Mrs. Mulholland could see her hands shaking before she folded them in her lap, out of sight. The waiter stood next to her, tray dangling from one hand. As if for protection, Vic crouched beside her mother's chair, one arm around her shoulders. Jane thrust wadded paper napkins into her hands and she began swabbing at Mrs. Mulholland's lap.

"No, no, don't bother with that. It's all right," Mrs. Mulholland said. Her two daughters' eyes, waiting, expectant, pinned her in place. "It's all *right*. Really. I'll be fine." There should be something to say, some wisdom to hand on, mother to daughter, like a relay race. But not, she saw now, the one thing she'd wanted to tell them—the one thing they did not want to hear. Forgiveness: it had been a foolish thought, after all. Sadness spread through her like an anesthetic. She felt as though she could hardly keep her head up, as though it would sink to the table, and her cheek rest on the cold, scarred metal in the spilled wine.

Alex gathered the family with her glance. "I don't believe George is coming," she said. Her voice sounded tired, as tired as Mrs. Mulholland herself. "Shall we go inside?"

Rising slowly, Mrs. Mulholland felt for her footing on the pavement, sticky with wine. Her shoes—scrappy, frivolous sandals designed to show off her ankles—were not to be trusted. She took Vic's arm, then held out her hand to Jane, who shook her head violently, whipping the pointy ends of her hair across her cheeks, and went to stand by her mother. Slowly they walked out, two by two, past the white and yellow sparks of chrysanthemums, the green laurel hedge, the beautiful enameled young men at the table by the door. Passing them, Mrs. Mulholland looked down at her ankles, the only part of her aging body she could still bear to see. How difficult it had been to accept that; only Tod had understood, those last years, moving slowly from window to window to close the bedroom shutters against the faint illumination of the night sky. I am a vain and foolish woman, she thought. Am I?

She felt a thump in the middle of her back. She turned.

Behind her stood Jane, hands on her small hips, squinting into the sun. "There. I got *everybody*," she said. "Now. Who's the—"

Automobile horns and a scream of brakes from the street beyond the iron palings drowned her out. There followed the dull crump of metal on metal, and then a volley of obscene words in male voices.

Mrs. Mulholland put her hands on her granddaughter's shoulders. "Never mind," she said, uncertain who the words were meant for. "Never mind."

The three women resumed walking. Ahead of them, between the pocked stone lions at the palazzo entrance, the afternoon waited among mahogany Holbeins and coolly glowing Bellinis in rooms that had been moved across an ocean stone by stone.

Eve and Adam, 1963

The real reason they sent me to stay with Clesta that summer was sex.

"How *can* we? With three pubescent girls in the house?" my mother would yell at my father sooner or later during every one of their battles. "That's why we *fight* all the time. It's the goddamn sexual tension!" The bedroom door would slam, and then the door to my mother's workroom, and we'd hear her loom scrape across the floor as she pushed it into a corner to unfold the rollaway bed.

So they parceled us out—my older sister, Rhoda, to be an arts-and-crafts counselor in the Poconos, my younger sister, Althea (Praise God, as Doc would say), to my grandparents down in El Paso—and went on a two-week package to Aruba for what my mother called a second honeymoon. But I heard her tell her friend Diana from Bryn Mawr that they were going there to work on the marriage, an activity that sounded drawn-out and dull, like two people bent over a dismantled car with its parts strewn all around it. I could help my great-aunt, they said; Doc, who'd kept house for Clesta from the day she married, was getting too old to do everything. I was glad to be the only one going to 110 Wesley Street, to have Clesta and Doc and Chinky and the whole glowing cave of a house all to myself, even though it meant there'd be nobody to hang out with. My only cousin in Bethlehem was a boy.

The Greyhound from Philadelphia was late; it was almost dinnertime when Chinky met me in the little foyer, gargling threats. He was a black Chinese chow with a seamed face and reddish popeyes. Doc and I hauled my duffel bag and my two suitcases up the winding stairs. Clesta's apartment took up the two upper floors of the house she'd inherited from her mean dead husband, huge and old, with a lot of dark wood. Doc's black face was shiny with sweat and his tongue kept flicking out to moisten his lips, like a minnow flashing back and forth.

Clesta hugged me, smelling of Ben-Gay. "Lilly," she said. "Lilly-Lil. You're bigger than last year."

My father's family runs to strange names for its women. Rose-Althea, my great-grandmother, named her daughters Clesta, Maude, and Eulalie; then, running out of steam, she named the boys Bob and John. Who's named Lillian these days? Still, I preferred my name to Rhoda's. I could insist on Lil, which sounded like a heroine of the Old West but was at least kind of rakish. There wasn't any nickname for Rhoda.

"Two and a quarter inches," I said. "Five-eight."

Behind me, Doc said, "She'll never be a beauty. Not like you were." He fingered his grey fringe of beard and sighed. "Well, time flies, is what it is. You get old, every fifteen minutes it's time for breakfast." He went back down the steps to the kitchen.

In the living room, late sun straight-armed its way through the half-drawn drapes. Two grandfather clocks, Big Gramp and Little Gramp, ticked unevenly, like two old men's voices going *tsk, tsk*. It was a room full of images. Family photographs stood on every table top, a century's worth of them: still, round-eyed sepia faces next to full-color children wheeling across summer grass. Chair legs carved in the shape of curved animal paws; blue-and-white tiles around the fireplace depicting Bible scenes; even the spoons at dinner would have handles twisted into cherubs. The dead husband's furniture, dark and looming, made the room feel cool even in summer. When I was small I liked to lay my tongue against the knobs on the wooden ladder-back chairs; they tasted dark and faintly bitter.

Clesta lowered herself onto the brocade sofa and patted the seat beside her. "So, Lilly. Tell me."

I talked about my new contact lenses and finally making the swim team and Rhoda's new boyfriend's hunter-green Camaro. Clesta's head quivered from side to side in little half-circles as she listened. When she laughed, her eyes had the mottled shine of old china, and there was lavender in the creases around them.

"You'll have a good summer. Where's my snivvy?" She thrust a hand between the seat cushions and brought up a crumpled Kleenex. "You can play with your cousin Bobby. You'll cheer him up." She blew her nose and tucked the tissue back between the cushions.

"*Play*. I'm a sophomore, Clesta." I wouldn't be fourteen until August—I'd skipped eighth grade the year before—but I tried to help people forget that. "What's the matter with Bobby?"

"Streetcar accident. Lost all but the big toe, on his left foot." She made a fist, then stuck out her thumb. "Now they're saying he'll always limp. Not badly, mind. But he thinks it's the end of the world, naturally."

My plan had been to work my way through the forbidden books shelved between stacks of sheets in the bathroom linen closet, with maybe an hour or two every afternoon watching soaps (also forbidden) in the kitchen with Doc. But I said, "Okay. I'll cheer him up." Thinking, he probably won't want to spend time with me any more than I want to spend time with him.

"On the other hand," said Clesta. Then she shook her head. "Open the drapes, will you, Lil?"

I pulled the gold rope with its little tassel, guiding the heavy linen past a clutch of photographs on the windowsill. A dead beetle lay next to them, its shiny shell the dark green-purple of an eggplant. Below me was Doc's garden, lush and wild, bordered by a high stucco wall. It had a lot of old-fashioned things in it—a sundial, wisteria, a grape arbor—and I'd always thought of it as the Secret Garden. "On the other hand, what?" I said.

"Oh. Nothing." Clesta's face had an inward look, as if she were listening to something. Then she smiled. "On the other hand there was a glove."

Laying a hand flat on either side of her, she pushed off from the sofa. Chinky stalked over (chows' back legs are completely straight) and butted her knees, and she scratched his broad, woolly head. "A-chink, a-chink, a-*chow*!" she chanted. He gazed at her out of small red eyes.

Recovering from dinner (roast pork with prunes; orange jello salad that tasted like children's aspirin), I lay on my stomach in front of the fireplace on a rug patterned with liver-colored roses. Doc and Clesta were in the kitchen doing the dishes. Screened from view by a large wing chair, I read the copy of *Lady Chatterley's Lover* that I'd found in the linen closet, its dust jacket removed, under a pile of lavender towels. I turned the pages quietly, sliding them between my fingers like hundred-dollar bills.

The new contact lenses burned. Remembering just in time not to dog-ear the page, I closed the book and lay without moving. It hurt to shut my eyes. In the lamplight, I could just make out the blue-and-white tiles around the fireplace: a terrified Jonah protruding from the mouth of the whale; Noah beside the Ark, with a row of animal heads hanging over its side; Moses parting the ocean into two neat scrolls. In a blue the color of ballpoint pen, the figures looked like the ones I used to draw when I was eight or nine, scratchy and angular, with legs like logs. I liked to browse through the Bible, the Old Testament, then draw the figures, nude if that fit the story at all, frustrated by the men's crotches because I wasn't sure what went there. I still wasn't.

My finger traced two figures on the lustrous, cold tile. Running, bodies curved like question marks, heads turned back toward what they'd left behind. Eve's arms were crossed over breasts as round and hard as the apple she held in one hand. Behind her, Adam, his chest smooth and narrow like my father's, wore a fig leaf curled across the fork where his legs split off from his body. On their faces, half-turned away, there was the most terrible longing.

I laid out my things on the cherrywood bureau: blue-green eye-shadow, lipstick, my mother's Skin Perfecting Cream which I'd filched from her dressing table. Then I pulled Bear and Bella Squirrel from the bottom of the duffel bag and propped them on either side of my pillow.

After I'd put on my yellow nightshirt with ON THE BOARD-WALK . . . IN ATLANTIC CITY across the front, I lay down in the green glow of the night-light and began to dream my way into the painting that hung by the bed, the way I always did at Clesta's. A girl stood at the beginning of a road that stretched into mist and trees. She wore a long, bunchy blue dress and a white cap. Across her shoulders she balanced a rod with ropes on each end holding buckets that hung down below her waist. She held each rope just above its bucket, and her eyes looked off down the road into the trees. She seemed to be straining towards them, but stiffly—as if she couldn't go there, only wait.

Something was wrong. This time I couldn't get inside. I lay wide awake, and my parents' angry voices seemed to come ribboning out into the dark. I was shaking underneath the sheets, cold even though the room was hot. I got out of bed and ran, breaking through the voices.

Clesta lay propped on half-a-dozen pillows with Chinky beside her, watching Johnny Carson. She never went to sleep before about three in the morning—something to do with her mean dead husband, but I didn't know what. She only slept on real silk sheets, with colors like the hearts of flowers: blue-violet, ivory, rose. The room smelled like mint and oranges.

"Lilly-Lil," she said, and moved some pillows over against the other side of the padded headboard for me. I settled into the cool, slippery silk, then felt something sharp. From underneath me I pulled out a large, bent tube of Ben-Gay. Peter Pain ran in terror across the front, with little wavy streaks behind him to show how fast he was going. I lay back among the pillows parallel to Clesta, with Chinky on her other side. There was a little pile of orange peels on the sheet between us.

"I couldn't sleep," I said.

Clesta flicked the remote control and Johnny Carson became a mouth soundlessly moving. "Journey-proud."

"What?"

"Journey-proud. That's what my mother used to call it. When we couldn't sleep the night before a trip, because we were too wrought up."

"I already made the trip."

"So you have. Well."

Chinky raised his gargoyle head, and I reached across Clesta to pat him. He curled his lip.

"It's the heat," said Clesta. "Makes him morose."

"It's hotter in Aruba." I sifted the pile of orange peels through my fingers, letting them fall onto the lavender silk one by one, then picked them up and started over. Behind Johnny Carson's head, as they broke for station identification, the word DIVORCE replaced HOLLYWOOD, huge white letters spread out across a green hill.

Clesta sighed. Her wide, flat breasts rose and fell under her nightgown. "Your father loves life. He's just—I've often thought, James is just one of the naturally joyful."

She picked up a picture from the night table and handed it to me. "His father was the same. My brother Bob. Even when he was a boy, you could see it."

In a long, narrow frame was a series of three pictures in which a sepia-colored boy sat on his sepia mother's lap. The boy had fair hair and large, dark eyes. First he was laughing; then crying, one round tear on his cheek like a blister; then twisting around to touch his mother's face. She was the same in every picture, unsmiling, in a high, scratchy-looking lace collar and pearl earrings.

Clesta put the picture back on the night table, leaning it against a photograph of Colonel Sam Hutchins in his Civil War uniform. "Journey-proud," she said again. "Now, *I've* never liked to travel. Even when I was younger, and never thought of dying in some strange bed and somebody having to come and fetch me home, all that trouble and expense." She squinted at me. "Did I ever say that poem for you?"

"What poem?"

She pulled herself straighter against her pillows.

> "'Here I am where I longed to be.
> Home is the sailor, home from the sea,
> And the hunter home from the hill.'

Now who was it wrote that? Anyway, it's carved on his tombstone. Good, isn't it?"

"It's okay," I said.

We watched Johnny Carson interview an irritable, balding fashion designer. The flickering light from the television clung to the edge of Clesta's profile, her slightly hooked nose and wild eyebrows. "Fashion!" she said. "A lot of fairies in New York City who don't want women to look like women." She sniffled. "Fashion is spinach!"

I was starting to feel sleepy. I slid off the bed.

"Now, before you go, where's my snivvy?"

I reached across and fished it out and handed it to her, then kissed her dry, soft cheek.

In my room I pulled the rough cotton sheets up over my face. I made my hand a fig leaf, moving it back and forth across the soft new hair until the feeling piled up, then let go. Afterwards my pelvis ached, a slow, sweet ache. I fell asleep.

At first all Bobby and I did was fish. I'd slip past the closed door where Clesta slept with a chair propped under the doorknob and feel my way downstairs in the half-light along the wide mahogany bannister. He'd be waiting in the little courtyard, his no-color hair in slept-on shocks, his eyes puffed from sleep. He'd stand there holding the two rods, his old one and his new one—a seven-foot graphite with a Shakespeare reel—straight up in one hand.

We'd go off in the morning coolness with the sun coming up red at the end of the alley. Bobby was tall for his age, even taller than me, and narrow all over. When he walked, he sort of wagged each foot at the ankle as he set it down. It made a little flapping motion, as if his jeans had ruffles at the bottom. On his left arm, just below the sleeve of his T-shirt, was a blistery scar like a lozenge, pink and shiny, where something had gone wrong with his smallpox vaccination when he was a baby.

We fished off the Lancaster Avenue bridge. We never caught anything. The first morning, Bobby'd popped out his spool and changed to six-pound test, as if he were expecting something. But after the second day, he didn't bother. I made him bait both hooks—my father'd always done it for me; I couldn't stand to stick my hand into the can of coffee grounds and feel for the humid, shifty bodies. My father doubled the worm up to pierce it quick and cast as soon as he could; Bobby would push the barb slowly through the worm's light-colored collar, then stop for several seconds to watch it curl and uncurl, hopelessly.

Then he'd hand me his old fiberglass rod and we'd cast out into the Lehigh River. I could do a snap cast, like cracking a whip. We leaned on the wall of the bridge with our butts stuck out to the traffic. The cement was cold and rough under my bare arms. Trucks trundled past, making the bridge vibrate and swing; I could feel the long drop down. Our voices went out over the water into the moist air. The nice thing was, we could talk without looking at each other.

"My folks aren't going to make it," I said one morning. "They sent me separate postcards." I lowered the tip of my rod until I felt the spoon swing, like a pulse at the end of my line. The low sun struck a dull sheen off the river.

I felt Bobby shrug. He said, "Maybe you're better off with just one." His father had died when he was six or seven, killed himself, my sister Rhoda claimed; but nobody in the family talked about how. They just said, died.

I started the retrieve. "Doesn't your mother have boyfriends?" I said. My father already had girlfriends; I'd seen him with one on Chestnut Street in March, when I cut school to go into Center City for *Lawrence of Arabia*.

"Nope. She'd never."

"Well, doesn't she—"

"In Zaire," Bobby said loudly, "know what they do? They eat termites live. Just pluck 'em right out of the air when they fly by. First they pull off the wings, then they—"

"Gross. Well, doesn't she go on dates? I bet she—"

"In China, they eat live monkeys' brains—"

My rod dipped. "Hey!" I yelled. I don't know why they call it a nibble, when it's more like a hand grabbing yours. The pull went right up through my arms; it felt as if my wrist was about to snap. My thumb found the catch, I opened the bail, and the line started traveling away from me fast. I could hear it sing in the guides.

"Set the hook!" Bobby yelled.

I yanked the rod up hard. The line went slack. I'd forgotten to close the bail.

"Must've just got snagged on something," said Bobby, who hadn't noticed about the bail. "Somebody's old tire, or an empty bottle. I'm hungry." He started reeling in. "There aren't any fish in this dumb river."

My heart tilted. "There *are*," I said loudly. "There *are* fish in there." I looked down into the blurry brown water. I was sure what I'd felt had been real. Maybe not pickerel or bluegill—but there *could* be carp: they can live in any water, even polluted. *Lighten up*, I could hear Rhoda say. What did I care whether we caught any fish or not? Probably Doc would refuse to cook them; or else he'd stew them up with raspberries and turnips. I started reeling in, fast.

Bobby looked at me sideways, his hand on the reel handle going slower and slower. "What would it feel like to be a fish," he said. "No arms and legs. No clothes. Just moving through the water with nothing."

He was hopeless. I stood my rod against the cement ledge and turned my back on him and the river. But in my mind I saw myself turning weightlessly in the water, feeling the separate mysteries of my own body, the things my body knew that I didn't. From the lunch sack I took a sandwich and an orange and a paper towel folded into a square. By the time I got halfway through it, my sandwich was gritty. Afterwards the orange was as good as water, sliding along the roof of my mouth.

We walked home in the noon sun. At the Moravian Seminary the sidewalk narrowed and we had to go single file. I dropped behind. Bobby walked with his head down, running the butt of his fishing rod along the iron fence with a dull clanging sound. His hair dovetailed into a point at the nape of his neck, like my father's. The scruff of the neck, Clesta called it—*I'll take you by the scruff of the neck*—but it was tender and pink.

The long mahogany-framed mirror in Clesta's bathroom delivered my body from the knees up, in a shiny turquoise bathing suit with a white stripe across it. Bobby had called to see if I wanted to go swimming—some friend of his had a pool. We weren't supposed to get there until after nine: the pool was lighted and all the kids liked to swim at night.

I twisted around to see the back. Being too tall at least meant I had long legs. Just below the backs of my knees, the mirror ended in a bench with elaborately carved arms and a curlicued base that continued around the room. At the other end an old-fashioned bathtub stood on clenched feet.

Maybe I should shave my legs? I opened the carved wooden door of the medicine chest over the sink; but of course there was no razor. Just Ben-Gay and Merthiolate and Pepto-Bismol and a lot of prescription bottles with yellowed, indistinct labels. Some of them had been there so long they stuck to the painted wood shelves. I opened a dark-blue glass jar of zinc ointment and smelled it. Instantly I saw my father on the beach at Humbird Lake, saw his white-coated nose flash in the sun. My joyful father who departed from his promises to make other promises, and then broke those. I capped the jar and put it back.

In the mirror I straightened the straps of my suit. There was nothing to be done about my flat chest or the way my shoulder blades poked out like chicken wings. At least Althea wasn't here to make fun of me, swaggering around with two rolled-up pairs of socks stuck in the top of her suit; or Rhoda, who never let me forget I was a year young for my grade, sliding a red-tipped finger around the bottom of her bikini. I undid my ponytail and my hair, the same no-color as Bobby's, fell over my shoulders. In the light from the window behind me, its paleness fanned out into a dozen blurry colors. I squeezed out my contacts and snapped them into their case. My face blurred just enough to be pretty. I pulled an old cotton shirt of my father's over my bathing suit and buttoned it. That looked weird, so I unbuttoned it. Then I thought about walking along the street with Bobby, and I buttoned it again.

"Praise God!" Doc said when I came into the kitchen. He cleared his throat with a soft pigeon sound. "Thought you was in the *bath*tub again."

Clesta turned from the sink to look at the two of us, Bobby and me, standing in the doorway in identical buttoned-up white men's shirts. With two soapy index fingers she smoothed down her eyebrows.

"Stay in there too long, your flesh'll shrivel up. Tips of your fingers get like walnuts." Doc held up one hand, pink palm out.

"You have her back by eleven," Clesta said to Bobby, as if he were my date.

Chinky saw us to the bottom of the alley, his black tongue hanging out from the heat. Streetlamps popped on in the muggy dusk. Our shower thongs clapped on the brick pavement and little bursts of insect voices sprang out from the hedges. I could smell honeysuckle. Some branches poked through the iron bars of the fence we were passing; I broke one and showed Bobby how to bite the end off a blossom and suck out the sweetness.

"Here." I handed him a stem with leaves attached. "I can't believe you didn't know that."

He sucked, then threw the empty blossom over his shoulder.

The pool was surrounded by a high redwood fence and filled with implausible turquoise light from floodlamps embedded in its sides. Kids were milling around, jumping in or getting pushed, pulling themselves out—all kids I'd never met, friends of Bobby's friend. Without my contacts they were all more or less duplicates of each other, frighteningly lifelike versions of Althea's Ken and Barbie dolls. They must have spent most of their days at the pool; they were an even caramel color all over, as if they'd been basted. On the diving board a girl in a hot-pink tank suit with her hair wrapped around her head like a bandage sat with her legs astride, talking over her shoulder to a boy. He sat close behind her, as though they were on a motorcycle. Bobby took me down to the deep end and introduced me to his friend, skinny Tim, all ribs, and a girl named Mattie who had the biggest breasts I'd ever seen on anyone my age.

"Jump in," Tim said. I hung around the cement apron at the edge of the pool waiting to see what Bobby would do about his foot. Would he keep his sneakers on, or his socks, or what? But he stood there talking to Tim about Richie Ashburn's RBI and other things I wasn't interested in until finally I shrugged off my shirt, stepped out of my thongs, and dived.

The water closed around me cool and sweet. I went all the way down until I touched bottom. Then I surfaced and swam for a while, not swim-team stuff, just sidestroke. After a while I saw Bobby in the shallow end, shaking the water off his hair.

Suddenly the lights went out. The water went dark, bottomless, a night sky pitted with stars. "Skinny dip!" yelled a girl's voice. Other voices joined in. "Skinny dip, skinny dip!"

All around me kids started taking off their suits. I hesitated. I'd never swum naked before, but I didn't want to look chicken. Treading water, I peeled down my suit. The wet fabric caught on my nipples and scraped my thighs. I pulled it over my feet. Water slid around my naked body like Clesta's silk sheets.

I found the side of the pool and clung there while I pushed my suit up over the edge and left it in a little pile. Letting go, I swam toward the shallow end, gliding through the water without moving my arms. I felt fast and light. The water fizzed across my body, over my belly, around my thighs. I felt part of it, at the center of it, fluid.

"Lil! Lil!"

The sound of my name fell like a warning in the darkness, little puffs of sound quiet as breathing. My feet found the bottom and I turned. In the vague illumination of starlight and far-off streetlight, Bobby crouched down like me, so that the water came to our armpits.

"Hi," I whispered.

"Hi."

A pause; then Bobby whispered, "Weird, huh? It feels weird."

"Yeah," I said. "Why are we whispering?"

I could hear the voices of the others in the deep end under the diving board, far off like the wrong end of a telescope. Out in the street beyond the redwood fence came the sound of someone whistling. It gave a shape to the darkness, that sound passing by. As if our names had been called, we stood up.

Bobby's chest was as smooth as Adam's, his thighs surprisingly large, round and solid. Water gleamed on them like silver ribbons. His penis pointed straight up, a little larger than a man's thumb. It *looked* like a thumb.

The back of my neck prickled. "Isn't it supposed to be bigger?" I said. I kept my voice level.

He reached for my hand. I took a step back, breathed slow and deep. He grabbed my hand and held it so tight my knuckles hurt. He pulled it towards him. "Here," he said softly.

It felt gristly, nosing my palm; but the skin was like velvet.

"Go on," he said. "You afraid?"

His balls felt strange. I didn't know what I'd expected—hard, maybe, and covered with short stiff hairs, like chestnut burrs. But they were soft and pouchy like a leather coin-purse.

We stood there in the humid night with the water lapping our knees. Gooseflesh ticked along my arms and across my chest. For a moment I knew all the things my body knew; then I pulled my hand away. I turned and dived. My stomach scraped the cement bottom. Pushing my heavy arms and legs through the water, I started back towards the deep end. The last line of Clesta's poem repeated itself over and over in my head; my arms and legs fitted themselves to its rhythm. *The hunter home from the, home from the hill.*

I didn't want it after all, the knowledge I'd been stalking. I wished, as much as I'd ever wished for anything in my life, that I could give it back. I dove down and swam underwater, keeping my eyes open so I could tell myself I wasn't crying. I moved along the bottom, slow and heavy. I stayed underwater all the way.

Happiness

"What do you mean, brother? I don't have any brother." Waiting for his shuddering heart to subside—when the phone rang he thought, absurdly, that it might be Maddalena—Thurston leans against the kitchen wall and looks out the window. Live oak and acacia stand motionless in the deepening twilight. Further down the slope, some low-growing bushes swagger back and forth, announcing the skunks who come up at night from the arroyo.

"—like I said," the voice on the other end of the phone continues, "I'm your brother. Half-brother, actually. Raymond P. Toledo." The voice is deep, with a threat of laughter—a salesman's voice, full of unearned bonhomie.

"I don't *have* any brothers," Thurston repeats. "Or sisters, for that matter."

"My mother's name was Bonnie Olenick. That's your mother, right? Our Aunt Marge in Cleveland told me how to get hold of you."

Our, indeed. "I'm an only child," says Thurston. With thumb and forefinger he rubs his narrow nose where his spectacles rest. "You've been misinformed. I'm sorry," he adds insincerely.

"You just moved out from back East, right?" the salesman-voice persists. "Grew up in Providence, R.I., right?"

"I grew up right down the road," Thurston lies, in precarious control now of his voice. "I've lived in South Pasadena all my life. Must be some other Calvin Thurston."

There is a pause. Then, "Sorry to bother you. Well. You have a nice day."

Thurston moves to clinch the deal. "Have a *great* day," he says, upping the ante, and hangs up firmly.

Coward, Maddalena would have said, *vigliacco*—or not said, just thought, loudly enough for him to pick up on it. Thurston sits down at the table with his elbows on the green-checked cloth. Tails up like question marks, two skunks rummage in the dusty leaves of a young eucalyptus. In the twilight the V-shaped stripe down each back is the blue-white of gardenias.

His mother left when Thurston was two; his father never spoke her name in his son's hearing, nor did he allow anyone else to. He got rid of all his wife's pictures (photos in their one album had irregular holes where her face or torso had been expunged) and died thirty-three years later without ever having mentioned her. Wherever she went, she has not been part of Thurston's life. And he does not even want to imagine the owner of the voice he just heard—meaty, red-faced, salt-of-the-earth—as any relative of his.

Thurston goes into the main room to get back to work. The guesthouse he rented illegally when he arrived in September stands on bare red clay between the main house and the lip of the arroyo. Inside, everything is hard and white and shining—the bare walls, the tile floor, the painted woodwork—like being in an enormous bathtub. He sits down on the sofa under the overhang of the sleeping loft. There are papers strewn all over: he has two dozen verses due at Holi-

Day Greetings next week. The month is October; the weather feels like August; Thurston is composing sentiments for Valentine's Day. There is a surrealness to this that exhausts him.

In the kitchen the phone rings; Thurston ignores it. Most of the fronts they've sent him are Female Spouse/Other: *For My Wonderful Wife/Better Half/Sweetheart/Darling/Honey/Wife.* He flips through the fronts that already have their visuals. The first, in the shape of two cutout rabbits (one in a red-ribbon bowtie) clearly calls for "Honey-Bunny"; the last, a color photo of a chimpanzee (in a red-ribbon bowtie) has him stumped. "Don't Monkey With My Heart?"

The phone is still ringing—fifteen rings, eighteen (part of Thurston's mind cannot help counting), twenty. He gets up and goes into the kitchen and yanks the cord out of the jack. Sitting down on the sofa again in the silence, he runs his fingers through his neat beard. The watercolor of two yellow rosebuds is easy; so is the pastel lace heart. He will not think of Maddalena.

Thurston the celebrant—vicarious partner in other people's births, loves, marriages, deaths, and the anniversaries thereof—goes to work.

By the time she left, moving herself and her houseplants (palm, grape ivy, devil's ivy, split-leaf philodendron—Thurston would like to forget their names but finds he cannot) closer to her practice in Warwick, Maddalena had accused Thurston, in her own language, of a number of things.

Fear of entropy. Fear of surprise. (*Timore d'entropia; di sorpresa.* He tried to point out the logical contradiction here, but Maddalena was unmoved.) Fear of marriage.

Well. Yes.

Another time she called him her guardian mole. Shouted at him to find someone else, someone who *appreciated* having her roadmaps in alphabetical order. Over the months of accusation her beautiful voice shifted its undertone from disbelief to doubt to despair. In the end it was she who found someone else.

Thurston's Mustang crosses the Harbor Freeway ("Oldest Freeway in America") and turns right onto Colorado. Every Tuesday he teaches an extension class at Pasadena City College, "Philosophy in Everyday Life," a last-minute substitute for its regular instructor, who left to join the Cistercians. He swings out into the lefthand lane to avoid a tow truck that has broken down. In front of him a VW Beetle bears a bumper sticker that says, "God Is Awesome." To his left trees skip past—acacia, palo verde, the eternal eucalyptus. Thurston can see them clearly—and beyond them, the woolly humps of the San Gabriel Mountains, the sunset—because the door on the driver's side of his car is gone. This afternoon, after a day struggling with "For My Honey-Bunny," he went outside to make sure the car would start and found the door neatly removed, hinges and all.

The students are always startled when Thurston appears. The sound of their voices shuts off and they swivel to face him with a swift collective scraping of stools. The room, a biology lab by day, is long and deep with rows of black-topped tables. Hard yellow overhead lights turn the brick walls the color of baked beans. In a corner at the front of the room is a human skeleton on an iron stand.

Thurston clears his throat. Through the high windows come the smell of gardenias and the sundown noises of the ducks on the little artificial pond outside, like far-off mocking laughter. "Good evening. The topic for tonight is"—he gives a quick glance down at his predecessor's syllabus—"Truth. How do we know what is true." Thurston explains, mentioning Plato, Spinoza (he has done his homework, one step ahead of his students), Boethius, turning now and then to write on the blackboard. The silence is not attentive, and as always he feels his carefully prepared lecture, like the sheaf of typescript in his lightly sweating hand, go limper and limper. The two Buildings & Grounds guys in the back row, as rosy and stolid as Thurston imagines Raymond P. Toledo to be, watch the skeleton with the expression of long-distance passengers regarding the back of the busdriver's head. Whenever Thurston pauses he can hear one of them cracking his knuckles under the table, the sound of popcorn popping. Others— Mr. Hitachi, a courtly retired gardener; silent Barbara Dahl, who has insisted that everyone call her Barbie; Mrs. Wentworth and Mrs. Meade, when their blue-grey heads are not gently sinking to their breastbones—tend to look at the skeleton and then away, their eyes alternating between it and Thurston in distracting ping-pong match fashion.

"And so we see that, as Plato maintains, the particular is simply— an accident. We are all accidents of history. Each and every one of us could just as well have appeared in some other place at some other—"

Mr. Gujarati is waving his hand.

"—time. Or not have—"

"Please. Professor." The dark eyes are brimful, the face suffused with a characteristic earnestness that Thurston on the one hand regards as spurious but on the other envies. Mr. Gujarati is studying to be a lie-detector technician. From their written assignments, which the class persists in treating as invitations to autobiography, Thurston knows far more about his students than he wants to. He knows that Barbie Dahl's baby is in difficulty, its brain growing while the bones of its skull do not; he knows that Mrs. Meade believes she has a guardian angel named Hugh.

"—not have appeared at all," Thurston finishes. "Yes, Mr. Gujarati?"

Mr. Gujarati gets to his feet. "What about HAPpiness?" His accent rocks syllables back and forth like small boats at sea. "How do we achieve to be HAPpy in this world of everyDAY? Happiness IS the natural END of man." He looks down on the blue head of Mrs. Wentworth. "And WOman."

Several of the others are nodding. George Boynton has stopped cracking his knuckles. Young Mrs. Dahl leans forward.

"Success is getting what you want," offers little Bettina Cheng, the technical writer. "Happiness is wanting what you get."

"Right on!" booms one of the Building & Grounds guys.

Thurston crosses the room and stands next to the skeleton. "The topic for tonight is not happiness. The topic for tonight is Truth." He has to shout to be heard over the crossfire discussion, people in the front row turning to speak to those in back, no one looking at Thurston. Happiness, they demand of each other, what makes people happy? "I tote this CURSE was for everyDAY life," Mr. Gujarati complains to Mr. Hitachi, agitation skewing his vowels. Thurston listens in dismay. He does not want to become involved with these people, these *particular* lives. After a few more minutes, fortunately, the bell rings.

When she lost the baby—was that when things went finally, ir-revocably wrong? February: in Thurston's memory the month after Maddalena's miscarriage presents itself as one long, white, wind-less Sunday, snow falling blankly, a dark room. Her vigilant sad-ness, which he could not touch. Her understanding, which neither of them mentioned, that he had been—not first, and not only, but nevertheless—relieved.

White roses shed their petals
To give your skin its hue;
Your lovely eyes have stolen—

"Your brother has telephoned. I have taken for you the message."

Charlotte, his Swiss landlady, is standing in the doorway of the guesthouse. She holds out a piece of paper with a phone number written in green ink. No, she cannot stay: in the morning they are coming early to paint the lawn.

Maybe he hasn't heard right. He spends so much time alone.

"The drought," she says, leaving. "The brown grass—ach! They paint a nice green, it is no longer a sore eye in the neighborhood."

Your lovely eyes have stolen—have stolen—

Thurston moves restlessly around the small space. He still has not recovered from tonight's class, when several students, led by Mr. Gu-jarati, renewed last week's demand for bumper-sticker wisdom, mak-ing mincemeat of his carefully prepared lecture on Beauty. His shoes tap on the tile floor. He tries the TV. On the religious channel a white-haired evangelist informs him, "We are blest here in America. Blest." Across the bottom of the screen a continuous tape repeats, TO MAKE YOUR VOW CALL 1-800-123-SAVE. Another channel of-fers an exercise, Confronting the Hidden Self, which calls for standing naked in front of a full-length mirror and asking yourself what you want out of life (the demonstration uses dolls). Thurston watches the news for a while—coalition forces gathering in the Persian Gulf— then switches off.

In the kitchen window the moon shines above the eucalyptus trees. Their pale trunks glow like nude flesh and their leaves cast a thousand separate shadows on the packed dirt. The moon is nearly full—one plump cheek ends abruptly at the jawline. To Thurston it has always seemed a female face. It is more than a little like Maddalena's. The concerned forehead; the wide cheeks; the eyes large and shallow-set. Her eyebrows were so fair that from any distance they seemed not to be there. Plato says that true beauty is without color or shape; but Plato never saw Maddalena. Her skin, Thurston remembers unwillingly, was shiny the way skin gets when you have a fever. It made you want to touch her. Half her clients—she was a physical therapist—refused to terminate when she told them they were done. Why would someone like that want to be with someone like him?

A breeze has sprung up; in the distance Charlotte's wind chimes offer their precise, impersonal music. Thurston finds himself still holding the piece of paper with the phone number. He folds it in half and puts it under the sugar bowl with the Warwick number Maddalena sent him, without explanation, the month before—two numbers he will never dial—and pulls his notebook towards him. Some rhymes are inevitable.

> Your lovely eyes have stolen from
> Forget-me-nots their blue

Halfway through Thurston's lecture on The Good, at a tap on the shoulder from Bettina Cheng, Mr. Gujarati rises. He reads from a piece of loose-leaf paper that shakes slightly in his hand. "'The secret of HAPpiness is this: let your interests be AS wide AS possible, and let your reactions to the things and PERsons that interest you be AS far AS possible friendly rather than HOStile.' Bertrand Russell."

"Right on!" cries Mrs. Meade.

"Happiness," counters Thurston, "is the perpetual possession of being well deceived. Jonathan Swift." Not bad for off the top of his head. Through the high windows comes the faint, derisive laughter of the ducks. He resolves to do some research.

The John Bull is designed in relentless imitation of a British pub, all rough-hewn dark wood and stucco. Squinting to adjust to the gloom, Thurston looks around for the red hat Toledo promised to wear. At the far end of the room, in one of the heavy wooden booths, it glows in the blue light from an overhead television set.

Toledo rises to greet him, shakes his hand too firmly. He *is* meaty. Tall—as tall as Thurston—and a good forty pounds heavier. Too heavy for the jeans he wears, which creak as he sits down.

"Call me Ray," he says, as Thurston knew he would. The hat, a red cloth baseball cap, says KETCHIKAN FISHFINDERS in white letters that curve around a map of Alaska. Raymond's hair boils out beneath the edges, a pale red nearly pink.

A brown-haired girl in a T-shirt with the Union Jack on it appears. They order Courage ale and, on Toledo's recommendation, something called bangers.

"So. My long-lost little brother. How do you like that." Toledo studies him, smiling. His eyes are the color of Windex, with white squint lines in the sunburned skin around them. Foam clings to his pale-red mustache; the mouth beneath takes on a womanly sadness when he stops smiling.

Older than me. It surprises Thurston that his mother was married before; he always assumed she'd married again after, figuring that she'd left his father for some other guy. "Well—Raymond. It *is* a surprise." This self-proclaimed brother, who wore him down— phoning every day, setting Charlotte on him—needn't think Thurston is going to get cozy. He is here, once, period.

Their ale arrives and Thurston takes several grateful gulps. It is cold and pleasantly bitter. For several moments they sit silent. The other diners, sequestered in their own high wooden booths, are invisible. Television sets crouch in the rafters in various parts of the room. Thurston watches ten tons of snow being trucked in from the Sierras as a Halloween treat for an orphanage in Van Nuys.

"What the hell. Tell me about yourself, Cal. I wanna know all about my little brother."

"Calvin," Thurston says stiffly. He is saved by the brown-haired waitress arriving with their food, sluglike grey sausages surrounded by a moat of mashed potatoes. Raymond does most of the talking, chewing with gusto and gulping ale, now and then extending his lower lip up over his mustache to clean it with little sipping sounds. He lives with his "girl" (four years older than he is, which makes her fifty-two) in the desert near Twentynine Palms. She runs a bar for the Marines at the base. He pans for gold (only three quart Mason jars of gold dust so far, but you never know) and collects turquoise and agate and quartz which he polishes in a tumbler and sells to jewelers in L.A.

"Don't know why she's so crazy about me. Pretty little thing like that," Raymond says cheerfully. "Says I make her feel safe. Can you feature that? You'd think the sun rose and set on my head."

His large hand, sweeping over the table, knocks Thurston's mug onto the floor. Raymond bends over, grunting, and wipes the floor with his napkin and Thurston's, while the waitress brings two more steins. He is what his voice on the phone told Thurston he would be, an affable bumbler, the kind of guy who uses half of your seatbelt on an airplane and says things like "lucky fucker."

"You got a girl? Woman, I guess we're s'posed to call 'em now." Raymond has noticed the gap in Thurston's earlier narrative.

"We—split up." Thurston hates himself for the hesitation, the slight quaver that Raymond doesn't fail to notice. Leaning forward, belly overlapping the edge of the table, he says to Thurston, "You love each other?" He sips his mustache.

Thurston shapes his lips for *no* but finds he cannot say it. He opens his mouth to tell Raymond to mind his own business.

"Well, hell then." Raymond leans back. "You could patch it up, Cal. What the hell. No statute of limitations on love."

Oh, for Christ's sake, Thurston thinks. On the television above Raymond's head, a man punches John Glenn on the jaw in the middle of a news interview. "The earthquake, that was just the beginning," he shouts as he is hauled away. "That was just a *sign!*"

With dessert (Raymond orders Piña Colada ice cream; Thurston, plain vanilla) they arrive at the subject of their (their!) mother. It is simple, and less painful than Thurston feared. She was killed a dozen years ago, on a houseboat in the Florida Keys; a motorboat cut it nearly in two while she was sleeping. It was her third husband's houseboat. He survived: he'd been sleeping aft, on a campbed.

"What're you gonna do?" Raymond says. "She didn't have an easy life. Some women, that's how it takes them. The thing Pop always regretted, she had to wear a cloth coat. He couldn't buy her sable like her girlfriends."

This guy could see a bright side to the Slaughter of the Innocents, thinks Thurston. He remembers one of the quotations he collected this week for Mr. Gujarati: Happiness, Tennessee Williams said, is insensitivity. It doesn't prevent the thought that Maddalena would have liked him.

"Now, Joetta and me. What we're gonna do, see, we're gonna save up a while longer. Then we're gonna buy a boat, a thirty-foot Chris Craft, say, or maybe a Sea Ray Express, and take it up the Inside Passage." His eyes shine like the ice cream on the ends of his mustache. "All the way from Seattle to Ketchikan, seven hundred and fifty-seven miles. What the hell. Glaciers, 20,000-foot mountains, waterfalls—thousands of 'em, like you've never seen. Sea otters. Whales. Brown bear and deer, they swim right up to the boat. Not another human soul, far as the eye can see. Just me and Jet."

For a minute, looking into the Windex-blue eyes, Thurston feels himself floating. He sees the shining reaches of dark water, the glaciers like luminous dunes, the sleek heads of the sea otters. He smells the snow-scented air, sharp as iodine.

At the end of the meal Thurston watches his half-brother count out far too large a tip (he insisted on paying for both their meals: "I asked *you*," he said, which was certainly true). Silent to express a disapproval that is clearly lost on Raymond, Thurston follows him into the warm night. His goodbye is tepid; to Raymond's parting "Call you!" he makes no reply.

But later, in the hot little sleeping loft, he dreams of turquoise and agate and gold plunging and tumbling in a huge iron cylinder, in which he, Thurston, is tumbling too.

Early in December Thurston finishes with Valentine's Day and starts on Easter. A Santa Ana blows dirt and dried-out eucalyptus leaves against the guesthouse windows as Thurston writes:

> Under an April sky of BLUE
> I met a little BUNNY—

He said to send this card to YOU
'Cause you're my Easter HONEY!

At PCC the class has finished with Values and moved on to Ethics. At least, that's what the syllabus says; as far as Thurston's students are concerned, the "major area of innarest" (Barbie Dahl, speaking for the first time since September, speaks for everyone) is happiness. The bland, accepting silence is gone; his students refuse the elegantly phrased thoughts of dead men. "What, PERsonally, do you BElieve?" Mr. Gujarati demanded of him the preceding Tuesday. Panicked, Thurston checked the pie-faced clock at the back of the room. He had no idea what, personally, he believed.

On the second Tuesday in December, in the PCC library before class, Thurston pursues happiness through the card catalogue. He riffles through journals with names like *Metaphysical Review* and *Mind*, comforted by the stalwart syllogisms, the footnotes spread across the bottom of each page like a safety net. Through the library windows comes the sound of hammering. They're beginning to put up bleachers for the Rose Parade, stretching across campus and down Colorado Boulevard, grey-painted, peeling, empty. Sunlight splashes the open pages of the *Journal of Speculative Philosophy*, drawing Thurston's eye to an essay on the delusional nature of human feeling. "Assume that an individual *I* believes *P* on the strength of evidence *E*, and that *E* is the sum of what *I* knows which pertains to *P*. Given the aforementioned conditions, it is phenomenologically pertinent that . . ."

This is what he's been looking for. This is how real philosophers sound. An undergraduate in a yellow blouse sits down across the table from him, rattles a box of Chiclets. Thurston copies out the formula for enlightening someone like Individual *I* who labors under the delusion that he is happy. *(1) Check I's life plan for: (a) commitment to mut. exclusive princ., (b) wanting thing humanly imposs, (3) etc.* The undergraduate flings her long hair smartly over her shoulders. *(2) Check I's method of fulfilling life plan: (a) imposs in context of I's society? (b) lacks essent. ingred?*

Thurston thinks of Ray. In the month since their first dinner together, meetings with his new-found half-brother have somehow become a once-a-week ritual, always for dinner, always at the John Bull. Raymond insists on paying. Cheerfully blind to Thurston's lack of interest, he brings maps and navigational charts and spreads them out over the table. His stolid tenacity is more compelling than passion. Despite himself, Thurston has learned to read the crackling charts with their hundreds of tiny numbers indicating depth, their pale-green warnings of hidden banks and shoals. He's begun looking forward to the maps—their few roads, their mottling of mountains and flat, amoebalike lakes. When the brown-haired waitress brings the bill he surfaces, feeling as if he's been somewhere else.

Ray keeps pushing for more—come out to Twentynine Palms, meet Joetta. Who knows, he's threatened, maybe they'll get married. "Might's well take a risk once and a while. What the hell. Life is haphazardous, regardless."

Thurston has declined. Absolutely not. He doesn't want to get in any deeper than he is already.

The cold light of the John Bull's TV sets is not kind to Joetta's fifty-two-year-old face, though Raymond doesn't appear to notice. The two of them sit opposite Thurston in the high-backed wooden booth, Raymond gazing at Joetta as she talks and stroking the little glinting hairs on her forearm. There is something fragile about her, something vulnerable, though actually she's on the plump side. She is wearing an orange dress with a halter neck; Thurston can see the start of her large breasts, a pleating of warm, tanned skin at each armpit. They disturb him, these little fans of flesh, they are more arousing than cleavage would have been. Around her neck is a string of Raymond's turquoises. There is a hesitance, something almost like fear, in her yellow eyes; or maybe it is just shrewdness?

"A little the worse for wear," she says to Thurston, reading his mind in that way women have, which he hates. Her drink is ginger ale, not ale, and she takes a long swallow. Her lipstick leaves a vermilion crust on the rim of her glass.

Thurston measures out a smile. He let Raymond talk him into this, but he never promised to enjoy it. "Well, Joetta—"

"Hey! Call me Jet. Any friend of Ray's."

She smiles warmly, but the yellow eyes make him feel cold. Thurston settles his spectacles protectively on his nose. Joetta reaches under the table and hauls up a red leather purse patterned all over with elephants lifting their trunks. She pulls out a brown paper bag and hands it to Thurston.

"Almost forgot. Merry Christmas early. Do they have persimmons in Rhode Island?"

Thurston looks into the bag: six or seven things that look like stunted oranges. He thanks her and sets the bag beside him on the wooden bench, where it can easily be left behind. The red leather purse shuts with a snap. He feels as if something has vanished into rather than out of it.

Ray says, "We figure now, maybe we oughta go to thirty-three, thirty-four foot—maybe a Bertram FBC. Right, Jet? If we're gonna live on it and all. What the hell."

"Thurston, you come visit and see my bar. El Dorado Bar and Lounge—that's its new name—Ray tell you? El Dorado," Joetta repeats, her bright lips tasting each syllable. "There's a lot we gotta do yet."

"Can you feature it?" Ray is still stroking Joetta's forearm. Thurston can see her nostrils flare, as if it irritates her. "Day and night on the water. Brown bear swimming up for your toast rinds in the morning."

"Some of those soft leather banquettes. A patio outside for dining under the stars. Those class of things. Ray's helped me out a lot already," Joetta tells Thurston. Her blued eyelids raise and lower at him like signals. "He's not like a lot of men. Tighter than skin on a grape—that was my ex. Took me for everything I had. With Ray you're safe."

"They make 'em tough enough for the open sea, not just the Inside Passage. What the hell. Maybe that'll be next."

Listening to two separate conversations, Thurston feels at first vindicated, then sad. He signals the brown-haired waitress, who brings his third stein: Ray and Joetta have left him nothing to do but drink. His half-brother is a fool, Thurston thinks, he's as deluded as poor Individual *I*.

Smiling at Ray, Joetta moves her arm out of his reach, puts her hand in her lap. Ray beams at her—this desert bandit, this carpetbagger of the heart. That's how it goes, Thurston thinks muzzily, how it always goes. He sees Maddalena's face. He's not going to let his brother—his *brother*, for Chrissake—get screwed. He takes a long draught of Courage.

Joetta leans across the table confidingly. "Ray knows how to say yes," she tells Thurston. "That's the most erotic word a man can say to woman—*yes.*"

Thurston cannot bear his brother's radiance a moment longer.

"Listen." He intends a shout but it comes out a whisper. "*Listen,*" he says to Ray, louder this time. "You think you're happy." He jerks his head toward Joetta, whose eyelids have narrowed to blue slots. "Well, lemme tell you. Lemme just tell you." The words come easily, the same speech he delivered to Mr. Gujarati two nights before. "Check your *life* plan, Ray. Unconditional—" he burps, "—unconditional commitment to two or more mutual—mutually exclusive desires—"

But these two are not listening with Mr. Gujarati's respectful, damp-eyed attention. Frowning, not quite decided, Joetta opens her mouth to speak. "Given these *conditions,*" Thurston shouts. "Given these—" It doesn't sound right. He spreads his arms for emphasis. The paper bag bounces on the seat beside him. "Consider— Consider the evidence *I*— No, the individual *E*—" Persimmons thud onto the wooden floor and roll out into the aisle. One rebounds off his right foot, hard.

Joetta decides on laughter. Her head tilts back; the tanned flesh of her bare arms shivers. After a second, Ray laughs, too. They lean across the table and say to Thurston, at the same moment, "Hey. Take it easy." Immediately they turn toward each other and hook their little fingers together.

"What goes up the chimney? Smoke!" they chant, in unison. Their eyes lock; their faces shine with laughter. Thurston might as well be in Rhode Island.

The next morning he stands in front of the full-length mirror. Morning sun fills the loft with glittering needles of dust that seem to pierce his eyeballs. Head aching, he confronts his naked image. Narrow shoulders and collarbone; two pale nipples and the extra third one just below the left, smaller than a dime (he thinks of the stories of one twin devouring the other in the womb); penis trembling lightly. He sees that he's forgotten to remove his socks.

401/331-6291: he doesn't need to look down at the paper in his trembling hand. Why can't he make himself dial it? Would Ray hesitate? Thurston's Hidden Self, gazing sternly back through its spectacles, seems to look past him. The neat brown beard looks odd above the white flesh, as if he were dressed and undressed at the same time. Ray wouldn't feel this crawling in his stomach when he remembered the dark-blue spring evenings, Maddalena's key stumbling in the faulty lock, her face pink with lies. And yet, there were the other times: Maddalena's big bed under the eaves, the shine of her breath coming toward him in the dark, the long chain of bones down her back, like knuckles.

Through the still morning air come the soft throat-clearings of mourning doves. Thurston thinks, Those we hate, truly hate, are those we have wronged. He understands that now. He looks around the spare, white loft, empty except for the chenille-covered bed and the reflection that asks nothing of him. Maddalena sent him this number; Maddalena does not hate him. Who, then, has wronged whom?

"Hey. Cal." Ray leans in through the space left by the door that Thurston still can't afford to replace. When he does, Charlotte told him last week, she's found the perfect car alarm: a synthesized voice that repeats over and over, I HAVE BEEN VIOLATED.

"Ray. What's up?"

Usually they meet inside the John Bull. Thurston looks around the parking lot. No sign of his half-brother's pickup.

"Listen," says Ray, and Thurston notices that his face is different—the lines deeper, the womanly set of the mouth more pronounced under the pink mustache. "You mind if we don't eat? Let's just walk, okay?"

A full moon keeps pace with the two men down Fair Oaks, its color deepening from silver to gold. Thurston breathes in the smell of gardenias and car exhaust, heady as the first drag on a cigarette. All week he thought Raymond wouldn't show. After Thurston's outburst on Thursday, he might have decided (Thurston contemplated the possibility with mixed feelings) that he didn't want a brother after all. Now, walking alongside him, Thurston is surprised to feel pure relief. They cover several blocks in a silence unusual for Ray. They turn—

Ray slightly in the lead—onto Del Mar, heading east, toward PCC. Finally Thurston says again, "What's up?"

Looking straight ahead, Ray says, "I left."

"Left?" In the moment before he understands, Thurston says foolishly, "Left where?"

"Jet. Joetta." Ray stands still. The brim of his red cap shades his face from the streetlamps; Thurston can't read his expression. "Comes down to it, she ain't the right crew for me. Says the trip's too dangerous. Dangerous! Doesn't trust me, is what she meant."

"I'm sorry," Thurston says. And he is: he feels his throat clamp shut.

"Yeah. Well."

Thurston puts out his hand, grabs Ray awkwardly by the elbow. Half-turning, Ray gives him a quick sideways look. Both men face front again. They walk like that for a few seconds, clumsily, out of step. Then Thurston lets go. Sadness washes over him. He feels as if he is seeing for the last time the shining ice, the sunlit tops of the mountains, the brown bears trolling in the clear air.

They pass the Pasadena Unity Church, with its marquee that spells out: EVERYONE WELCOME. CREATE A NEW YOU. Ray is still a half step ahead. He walks with his head down and his hands in his pockets, clicking something. They turn down a side street devoted to condominiums. The grass between the sidewalk and the curb has been painted green, like Charlotte's; in the moonlight it doesn't look bad. Someone has wrapped the trunks of the fig trees in aluminum foil and tied each one with a large red bow. Thurston is reminded that Christmas is only two days off: Holi-Day has him doing Mother's Day cards now.

"What'll you do?" he says.

Ray is silent. For a moment Thurston thinks he's about to ask him to move in with him, share expenses, they're brothers after all—but of course Ray does no such thing. He draws a long breath. He says, "My cash is all tied up in the bar. I had to sell the truck, the tumbler and all. Everything. I'm gonna hitch to Seattle, pick up a boat second-hand." Ray's face is still shadowed by the hat brim, but his voice is the ghost of his old voice.

"You're going anyway?" Something more than relief wells up in Thurston, a tickling so strong it might be joy.

"What the hell. Won't ship, won't keep. Can't head for *someplace,*

I'm cooked. Might as well be Ketchikan. Hell, maybe I'll keep going, maybe go on up Prince Rupert Sound to Valdez."

On Colorado they turn right, heading east again. Bleachers for the Rose Parade line both sides of the street. In the moonlight they look like the skeletons of something. The two men walk in silence for several blocks; then Ray stops and turns to Thurston. He pulls his hands out of his pockets. For the first time, he smiles.

"Cal. You take care, you hear?" He puts something into Thurston's hand. A polished stone, oval and warm from Ray's grasp, almost the color of moonlight. "Rutilated quartz. For Maddalena," Ray says. He punches Thurston lightly on the arm. "Be seein' ya."

And then he is striding away down Colorado Boulevard in the direction of the freeway.

"Hey! Ray! You've got my address," Thurston calls after him.

Ray turns and, walking backwards, holds up two fingers in a V for victory. Then he turns around again.

"You've got my number," Thurston shouts. "Call me!"

He watches his brother moving east, moving fast, until he is a tiny figure between the stark, spectral rows of empty bleachers. Thurston is left standing in the moonlight in the middle of Colorado Boulevard, three miles from where he left his car. The stone in his hand has grown cool, and his palm tingles, as if the stone has given off something his skin is absorbing. He opens his hand. It glows imperfectly, a dozen flaws like tiny shining wires trapped inside. He stands looking down at it. The ringing of the crickets is like faint incessant sleighbells on the warm air.

What the hell, Thurston says to himself. He turns and starts to walk back the way he came.

Urban Fishing

Jean watches her stepdaughter run down the steps to the ledge along the canal. Half an hour ago she was white with fear, stretching her arm out stiffly for Jean to hold while the doctor cut away her small pearly thumbnail and the infected tissue underneath. Her blood fell in bright round drops on the tile floor, not scarlet but the deeper color of a cardinal's hat. She didn't cry then. But afterwards, out in the corridor, when the nurse came toward her with the needle for her tetanus shot, she screamed, "Not here! Not here!" The nurse didn't understand. "You have to have it in the shoulder. That's the way it's done," she said. Her voice crackled as if it were starched. But Ellen meant: not here, in the hall, where strangers can see.

Now she is fine. She looks over the edge of the low wall, leaning alarmingly. "The fish," she demands of her father. "Where are the fish?"

"The water's polluted," Charles says. "If you see anything, it'll be dead."

Jean says quickly, "All the fish saw the water was getting dirty and bad to live in. So they turned around and went back."

Like all six-year-olds, Ellen is intensely interested in the two great themes of death and sex; but only in a theoretical way. No concrete demonstrations. "So they were saved," she says with satisfaction.

The three of them sit down in a row on the ledge. Across the canal the narrow pale houses are packed tightly together in the smoky light of early spring. It's warmer today, warm enough to sit outside while they wait for the good restaurant across the canal to open for lunch. A long winter; and grey. After nearly two years in Buffalo, Jean is still homesick for the green of Seattle, gleaming dully even in winter, for the smell of woodsmoke caught in the shimmering net of rain. The lakes there were full of fish, saved at the last possible minute by a water reclamation bill.

In the absence of fish, Ellen wishes loudly for a boat. As if in answer, one appears far down the canal to the left, crawling toward them over the flat, dark water. Two figures in it, too far away to show their sex, seem to be fishing. What on earth could they hope to catch?

While Ellen strains to see and Charles looks inward, pondering some intricacy of the tax laws, Jean drifts backward into memory, which lately draws her more and more. Long years of Catholic school have left her with an excellent memory, but it only works on explicit instruction. The price she has paid is the loss of that memory that works without you, selecting randomly and wonderfully, so that ideas and sensations lodge unexpectedly in your mind like a fishbone caught in your throat. Lately, though, the past has begun to visit her uninvited. Maybe because, at thirty-five (which she thinks of, biblically, as half-way through her allotted span), the sense of a boundary in front of her opens up the space behind.

It was at the end of her twenties, when the future was still an open (though somewhat stormy) sea of possibilities, that Jean met Rob on the outdoor escalator going up from the parking lot to Padelford Hall. Her first day on campus; her first day as a somewhat overage graduate student. Dazed by the long, dreamy motion up through evergreens and rhododendrons, she didn't notice anyone behind her. Later he told her he was captured by the masses of Rapunzel hair reaching down her back almost to her waist—snared by its pale ropes.

He spoke to the backs of her knees. "Hello," he said, and she turned and looked down at him. "Rob Stieglitz. It's Pennsylvania Dutch—Pennsylvania German, really. Means 'goldfinch.'" He *was* large and golden, tawny all over; his bare arms looked as if, if you touched them, they would feel like plush. Since he was married, and since Jean had resolved, after her divorce, never to do to another woman what had been done to her, they became friends.

Rob was a poet. He was also, it turned out, a tenured professor in Jean's department; but since he paid little attention to this fact, preferring to see himself as an artist who sometimes taught English to make ends meet, it didn't get in their way much. Like all the poets in the Pacific Northwest, he worked in the shadow of Theodore Roethke. No matter what you saw, Roethke had seen it first; no matter what you did, Roethke had done it better.

"Christ." Rob looked gloomily into the acrid coffee at the Student Union. "If only the government would pay poets not to produce, the way they do farmers." It wasn't only Roethke's ghost, but the air of the Northwest, that caused his periodic writer's block. Seattle, hotbed of mediocrity, the upper left-hand corner that they always used to cut off the TV weather maps in New Jersey. Life there was too pleasant, too easy: the mountains, the water, the emptiness and quiet.

"There are two kinds of people in the world," Rob intoned. "Those that own RV's and those that don't. The latter can be divided into two subcategories: those who know RV stands for Recreational Vehicle, and those who don't." Since Rob viewed the poet as something like an old-fashioned metal meat grinder—experience in at one end and poetry out at the other—the blandness of life in the Northwest made him sardonic.

During one of his constipated periods he took Jean to the Amazon Exotic Bird Shop out on Route 99. Birds, he thought, might break the spell. Route 99 looked to Jean like a transplanted piece of New Jersey, an endless Paramus of used car lots and discount centers. Tucked between the Twin Teepees Restaurant and a bowling alley, the Amazon Exotic Bird Shop was easy to miss. It was run by Seventh Day Adventists and kept peculiar hours. Rob had it all down, though. They drove straight to the door, and it opened.

Inside was one of the foulest smelling, noisiest places Jean had ever seen. She understood at once why Rob's wife Evelyn refused to go there. Birds everywhere, small ones in cages stacked against the walls and on a table in the middle of the room, large ones, uncaged, on stands scattered around. One enormous bamboo cage held two bright-and-dark birds with beaks like scimitars.

Jean edged past a large green parrot on a stand near the door. It made a hissing sound, exactly like a snake, then shouted something unintelligible. All over the store birds warbled, gargled, creaked, and groaned, scribbling the air with sound. Rob looked around at Jean. "Aren't they great?" he shouted.

A large black woman emerged from the gloom at the back of the store. She nodded at Rob as you do at someone you recognize but don't want to get mired in conversation with. Rob made the rounds of the place, stopping here and there to gaze intently at one bird or another. Jean followed, skirting the larger, more vicious-looking ones. The really awful thing about being a bird, she thought over the din, would be that you could never lie down.

When Rob had absorbed whatever it was he'd come for, he headed for the door. As they passed, the large green parrot uttered another string of syllables. "What's he saying?" Jean shouted at the woman.

"*Toujours la gloire,*" she shouted back.

Maybe because he needed stuff for the meat grinder, Rob traveled a lot, going off suddenly and unpredictably. Jean had always thought of poets as sitting in their garrets, waiting for the muse. But Rob didn't like to sit and wait for life to come to him. Go to meet it, he'd say. Once he went to Chios because, he said, he needed the lemon-colored light of Greece. (The Guggenheim Foundation footed the bill.) Another time he stayed for a week in a little town in Florida where all the residents were former circus performers. "You're having breakfast in this little diner," he told Jean when he got back, "and first a pair of Siamese twins comes lumbering in. Then a midget. Then an enormous fat woman in spangles." He loved finding Walden Pond under construction or Niagara Falls turned off. Evelyn stayed at home with the boys.

Whenever he went anywhere, Rob sent Jean a postcard. (Not letters; he was the world's worst correspondent, he told her. All his friends from high school and college and graduate school had slipped away because of it.) From Vienna he sent a museum postcard of one of Egon Schiele's erotic nudes. "This guy knew what it feels like to be in a woman's body," he wrote. Another card showed a restaurant interior, starched and glittering and hung with a banner that said, "Greetings from the Petroleum Club, Atop the Fourth National Bank of Wichita."

Once a year, in early summer, Rob took Evelyn and their two young sons back to the little town near Lancaster that had sent him off in triumph, eighteen and golden, to play football at Penn State. Rob the contradiction in terms, the living oxymoron: a poet jock; a Don Juan who believed in true love. Jean imagined how it must have been. *Why I know you,* he'd have thought when he first read Roethke, the book small in his large hands, the blue-and-gold October afternoon sharp outside. Not *déjà vu* but a piercing familiarity. *I know you.* In his office now he kept his senior photograph, the year he was the star: crouched to spring, huge padded shoulders; and then the eyes, the tender Adam's apple. Every June, Jean got a card with a photograph of the Lancaster town hall.

Their relationship was like a seesaw. When Jean was free, Rob was married; later, when he got divorced, she was involved with Charles. Within these large arcs, smaller ones. On the days when his bare arms in a T-shirt gave her a jolt of desire, Rob's mind was elsewhere, wrestling with some tangle of syntax. When he was feeling lustful, she was in control, practicing the kind of responsibility the nuns had taught, fulfilling the female mission to keep male urges within bounds (if you must sit on a boy's lap, say in a crowded car on the way to a C.Y.O. dance, put a telephone book between you).

The university was a narrow world where everyone took a mildly prurient interest in everyone else's sex life. Rob usually knew who Jean was sleeping with. He'd take her to Ali Baba's on Pine Street for falafel and needle her about it, accusing her of madly squeezing a right-hand foot into a left-hand shoe.

"What?"

"Lewis Carroll. Don't you read anything? These guys aren't your style. Butnik. Messer, for Christ's sake."

He had a point. Jean thought of David Butler: limp, languorous pose, circular turn of phrase. In bed he said the things he imagined they said at Harvard, things like, "Now I know what a cellist must feel like, playing on a rare and beautiful instrument." Shimshe Mesara was the opposite extreme: an Israeli, a *sabra*, studying physics on a government grant. His idea of technique was to chase her around the sofa in her apartment, grabbing at whatever protruded. Making love, he watched himself in the mirror above her bureau.

Once Rob dug into the files from the English-as-a-second-language course and gave Jean one of Shimshe's freshman compositions. "This is the brain that goes with that brawn," he scrawled across the top. She'd had enough of Shimshe by that time anyway, tired of being black-and-blue in odd places.

At first Jean was afraid that one of them, she or Rob, would say something to push them over the line separating friendship from whatever lay on the other side. But gradually she saw that they might already have what they needed from each other. Qualities that in a lover would frighten or disturb her, in a friend were simply piquant. Rob's periods of withdrawal, when he wasn't around, didn't return phone calls or pick up his mail (Genius at Work) were okay because they weren't lovers. As for Rob, he could write her poems full of references to plains, skies, and calm eyes, secure in the knowledge that he committed himself to nothing.

The second fall, in September, she took him home to meet her landladies. Mabel was in the side yard under the Blue Atlas cedar, watering the flowers with a green plastic watering can. "Pleased to meet you, young man," she said, her face crinkling along its network of wrinkles. She thrust out a hand in a blue wool mitten. A wool helmet to match was pulled over her thick white hair, though it must have been seventy-five degrees and the sun shone down through the heavy fronds of the cedar.

Mabel took them into the upper part of the house to have tea with Inez in the parlor crammed with keepsakes and rubbish and stacks of old newspapers and *National Geographics*. The corners smelled of cat.

Mabel grabbed the seat next to Rob on the sofa; but that allowed Inez to sit opposite him crossing and recrossing her knobby, veined legs in their Bermuda shorts. Her hair, which would have been as white as Mabel's if she hadn't dyed it, sprang out around her head like copper wire.

"Young man." She leaned toward Rob. "What are your prospects?"

Rob didn't even look startled. "I could be the finest poet of my generation. Or the worst. Probably somewhere in between. Meanwhile, I have two boys, two dogs, and a lot of debts."

"Wife?" Inez rapped out.

"Yes, ma'am." Her face fell; then she brightened. Jean, afraid she was about to ask pointedly about Evelyn's state of health, said quickly, "How are the cats? I haven't seen Hector around lately."

Mabel jumped in with a catalogue of Hector's recent exploits, and between them she and Jean headed Inez off into a conversation about Cat People and Dog People.

Both women pressed food on Rob and Jean at intervals, uttering little chirps and clucks, aggressive as mother birds poking worms down young throats. When Jean had moved into the first-floor apartment, Mabel and Inez had quickly found out she was an orphan, raised by a grandmother now also dead; they'd adopted her immediately. Now they beamed at her for producing this great golden bear of a man, someone new to feed.

At sunset Jean walked Rob out to his car. Looking back, she saw Mabel and Inez standing side by side to watch him go, two old women in the doorway of the house they'd shared for two-thirds of their lives.

At the end of that fall, Jean began one of those times when, as Mabel said, you just keep putting one foot in front of the other. It wasn't the weather, though that second winter seemed worse than the first. In that latitude the light (not the sun) came at eight in the morning and left at four in the afternoon. Houses and trees were drifted over with rain; rain seemed to lie or float in the air rather than fall, a ceaseless fine mesh. Jean watched through her living room windows as Mabel came to set a dish of beer under the Blue Atlas cedar, for the slugs.

"You have to keep after them," she said. "They just take over, otherwise."

"Once," Inez announced, "I saw two slugs mating."

"What was it like?"

"Just what you'd expect," said Inez darkly.

Jean watched the slugs converge on the saucer of beer from all directions, an eerie lumpish procession. They drank and died. Jean hoped they died drunk, from a surfeit of pleasure, like Elizabethan lords.

She lay awake listening to the sound of dogs barking in the empty night streets. She felt as if her blood weren't contained in her veins, felt it humming, sloshing around loose in her body. She hadn't been this rootless, this lost, since the end of her marriage, when beautiful, quicksilver Jimmy went off with someone new, and Jean, who was known, was left behind.

Now, drifting ungrounded from one man to the next, she felt as if, in folding the tent of their marriage and stealing away, Jimmy had condemned her to a life of wandering. You're this, you're that, her lovers told her. This is you: a cello, a cold-hearted bitch, a born mother. Jean never recognized herself in these portraits. She was tired of it, tired of new bodies that sprang small blunt surprises, tired of searching for small areas of virginity.

Rob saved her. Because they weren't lovers, they could say things to each other, not needing to choose their time, just blurting. Once she put her face in her hands and cried. He patted her knuckles with his napkin. He held onto her hands. "Listen, Rapunzel. I think you're terrific. What do you say we go get a falafel sandwich?"

That was the time when Jean was most tempted. Rob was still married; but he and his wife had decided to be open about affairs. "It's a mistake," Jean told him. "You'll split your marriage apart. It never works." But they'd tried everything else. They'd even seen a marriage counselor for a while, but she fell in love with Rob, so they stopped. Rob and his wife were married for life, he said, because of their sons. He tried to think of the long haul. " 'In this bitterness, delight,' " he'd quote gloomily, " 'lies in flawed words and stubborn sounds.' "

Jean didn't want to risk what they had. Their friendship was the thing keeping her sane.

In the third autumn of their friendship, the seesaw shifted again. Evelyn fell in love with one of her lovers; she left Rob and took the boys.

When Jean went to his new apartment for dinner (overcooked fish and soggy Brussels sprouts), the bathroom floor was covered with water, and dozens of socks, crumpled into little balls, perched on the wooden drying rack in the bathtub like so many blackbirds on telephone wires. Over dinner, Rob talked a lot about bones. To distract him Jean asked what he thought of a recent collection of poems by a famous journalist.

"He thinks writing poetry means you get to use adjectives," said Rob. But his sneer was listless, without conviction. Little dark flecks muddied his golden eyes.

This might have been a romantic dinner à *deux*, though Rob had forgotten to buy candles and they ate under the baleful glare of the kitchen ceiling light. But Jean had begun an affair with Charles: a serious affair, grown-up, monogamous. She'd taken to wearing her hair in two braids wound around her head like a coronet. Charles, who didn't leave things to chance, who liked to know where he was going, hesitated about marriage. Jean knew that when he made up his mind he would be sure. Each day with Jimmy had engaged her so completely, had been so full of surprises, that she'd never looked ahead to see where they were going.

Rob sneered at Charles, whom he'd never met. "How can you even *like* the guy? A lawyer. An I.R. fucking S. lawyer, for God's sake." He believed a crime committed against Internal Revenue wasn't a real crime—more of a Robin Hood gesture. Jean didn't disagree, though she didn't air this view to Charles.

She said mildly, "He's a good man. He's—responsible." She thought of Ellen, whose mother had been too much a child herself to raise one, Ellen who fit exactly into the curve of her arm. "He's a good father."

"Yeah, I can just see him. Red face. Attaché case. Rumpled Brooks Brothers dignity." The thin, sharp current of sexual anger had always run underneath the surface of their friendship. Was it only that Rob no longer had the energy to keep it down?

His face was like a fist. She couldn't be angry with him when he was so miserable. She reached for his hand; the golden hairs on his arm shone in the bleak fluorescent light.

"It's *hard* to go forward, Jeanie."

She wanted to put her arms around him. To say, "It's all right. You have me." Instead she said, "I know."

"I hate *dating*. It's like sitting there behind the steering wheel, reading your owner's manual, when all you want to know is where the windshield-wiper button is. I hate living alone."

"I know, Rob. I remember. It's as hard learning to sleep alone as it was learning to sleep *with* somebody."

Running his finger around and around the rim of his wineglass, Rob asked, "Are you sure you want him?" But he didn't try any more to dissuade her.

The following spring Charles was transferred to Buffalo. After he'd been there two months, he called Jean and asked her to marry him. Thinking in equal parts of him and of Ellen, whose small vanilla-smelling body she perhaps coveted more, Jean said yes.

She withdrew from the University, got her passport, bought decent luggage. Mabel, though she'd never met Charles, was pleased because of Ellen. "People who didn't grow up in a family need to build one," she said. Inez took Jean aside for a discussion of the facts of life. As far as she was concerned, Jean's having been married before simply argued a stronger need for the lecture. She was clinical. (Mabel had told Jean the story of Inez's hysterectomy. When they uncovered her in the operating room, they found scrawled in eyebrow pencil across her belly: "Take what you must, but leave my clitoris.")

On the day her plane left, Jean called Rob. She listened to the phone ring and ring, watching early morning light filter through the branches of the Blue Atlas cedar and play along the ground like water.

"It's me."

"Jean." His voice said he wasn't alone. "What's up?"

"I don't know. I just—I wanted to say goodbye."

"Listen. I hope everything is great for you, Jeanie." He didn't point out that they'd already said goodbye. "We'll write. Well, no. Maybe I'll come and see you." She knew he wouldn't. Even the lure of a place he'd never been before wouldn't be enough to compensate for spending a week with Charles. She could feel the itch of tears gathering behind her closed eyelids.

Silence. She said, "Am I doing the right thing? Rob? Should I go through with this?"

But Rob only invoked Roethke, a verse he'd recited for her many times before.

" 'My dearest dear my fairest fair,
　　Your father tossed a cat in air,
　　Though neither you nor I was there.' "

His voice blurred, maybe only with sleep. "Go to meet it. I'll miss you, Rapunzel."

They said goodbye then. Jean sat holding onto the buzzing receiver, watching two early squirrels wind up and down the wavering trunk of the Blue Atlas cedar.

"Look! Jean!" shouts Ellen. The boat is near now. At the tiller is a squat Oriental woman with cropped pudding-basin hair. The other figure is a bearded man in a padded jacket. When the woman hooks something with her pole, the man makes a scooping motion, pulls it up in his net.

"Why, it's bottles," says Charles, turning to look, startled out of his reverie by Ellen's shout. "It's bottles." A light moist breeze lifts his thinning hair and moves Jean's own hair, short now, against her face.

The man and woman examine their catch each time, putting some in the boat, throwing others back into the pewter-colored water. They back up, using the motor, back and fill, covering the breadth of the canal.

"How could it possibly pay them to do that?" Charles must be calculating the cost of the gas. "Even with the deposit."

The boat pulls level with them and the bearded man waves, then takes a swallow from a bottle very like the ones he's been pulling out of the water. The woman turns her face up to the pale March sun and closes her eyes. They fish like fishermen everywhere, for the sport, for the chance to get out on the water.

The second half of life, Mabel used to say, is picking up the threads you've laid down in the first half, trying to coax from them some sort of pattern. Jean watches the restaurant across the canal fold back its shutters one by one. After lunch, they'll go downtown to Strawbridge's and buy Ellen another plastic horse, because she was so brave.

They get up to cross the bridge.

Dancing Fish

The first time his brother died, Seth was fifteen. It was November of 1973—Raphael's first weekend home since he'd started at U Mass—and Seth woke early from a dream of smooth, dark, faintly bitter skin, of warm breath across his ear. He swept off the striped woollen blankets and pulled out the sticky mess of the top sheet to roll up for burial in the bathroom hamper. Standing naked on one leg, then the other—Rafe had mentioned in one of his letters that he, like Nietzsche, slept in the nude now—he dragged on jeans and an old green Saint Jude's sweatshirt. It was warm for this early in the morning, too warm for November. He made a chink in the blind with two fingers. There was dense white fog where the road should have been. From the kitchen below came his mother's voice, singing. Built by his father from a kit the year Seth was born, the house leaked sound through every cedar pore—a house in which it was impossible to be alone. *My feet could step and walk,* Louisa's voice informed her son through the floorboards, *my lips could move and talk.*

Hugo, the aged basset hound, lay in his usual spot in the hall, blocking the stairs. As Seth stepped over him, he lifted his face with its built-in expression of grief, then turned back to Raphael's closed door.

"I wonder will this—Lucy—will she like red meat and chocolate, do you think?" At the sink, Louisa Godburn held a sheaf of bright green lettuce under the faucet. The room smelled of tarragon and basil and overripe bananas. A fat fly that had overshot its lifespan bumbled against the fog-filled windows.

"Why not?" Hearing the name, Lucy, Seth realized that that was who his dream had been about. Though Rafe's letters—notes, really, and only two of them since September—had barely mentioned her, just her age, almost twenty-two, and her skin, the color of which his parents did not yet know about. He got a box of cornflakes from the shelves that lined one wall and sat down at the wide oak table.

"And then, should we eat in here, or—" Louisa turned around. Her face was rosy with anxiety; her greying hair had frothed up from running wet fingers through it.

"Mother. The fog'll clear soon. Busdrivers know how to handle it, anyway."

Frowning, Louisa turned back to her lettuce. She shook each leaf, patted it tenderly with a thin white cotton towel. While he ate, Seth could hear her humming, low-voiced, into the soapstone sink. The Godburn family never talked about what Raphael had done the winter before; maybe that was why it never left them, why Rafe himself was always there somewhere, on the edges of their minds, even when he'd gone two hundred miles away. Only Louisa, once in a while, would look as if she were on the verge of saying something: her full, chapped lips would part; and then she'd sing, instead.

Hugo clacked carefully across the linoleum that he could no longer see and crept under the table. There was some moaning as he settled—Seth saw his mother wince—and then the sour smell of dried pee drifted upward. Louisa sat down across from her son and said confidingly, "We need a helium pump."

"A helium pump."

"Whatever they're called." She reached over to open a grey card-board box. It was filled with uninflated balloons, all blue.

"Won't he be surprised? Remember that time at India Point Park, when you boys let off all the balloons into the air? I want them to float," Louisa said. "*Float*. Run ask your father do we have one. He wanted you out there to split wood—I forgot." She looked at Seth's half-empty bowl. "Better go now. You know how he gets."

Seth stood up. Usually when his mother got into this mood, the mood his father called Dear Nonsense, it irritated him; today, for some reason (oh—Rafe was the reason, Rafe coming home), it was catching. Grasping his mother's solid forearms, he pulled her out of her chair. He began to dance her, laughing, protesting, around the oak table. We two are the ones who are here, now. *Here* (two, three) *now* (two, three) *in* (two) *this room*. Louisa's feet in slippersocks slapped the floor. From beneath the table came a low, croupy sound that was almost a bark.

"Go home," Francis Godburn said to Hugo, who had followed Seth outside and was preparing to lie down among the split logs. "Mother of God. *Home*."

The ax came down with a hollow report and the last hickory log fell away in two neat halves that clattered on the stony ground. Head down, Hugo turned and began to haul himself slowly up the slope to the house.

"Time he was put down." Francis Godburn pulled a yellowed handkerchief out of his pocket and wiped the back of his neck, then his face. Raphael's face (though Rafe denied it): dark eyes set deep, a long dimple beside the full, almost tender mouth. Eight-thirty in the morning ought to have been too early for a man who worked the three-to-eleven shift; yet between them lay a small sea of split hickory and oak and maple. The ones that had fallen raw side up were pink and naked-looking.

A long, even stack of wood stretched waist-high between two birches where the woods began. "We'll divide it here," said Francis Godburn. He shoved his handkerchief into a small chink mid-way along the stack. "That's your half." He gestured at the side where Seth stood. "This is mine. See whose side is the highest, time we're done."

"Okay," said Seth, the first word he'd spoken. Everything has to be a test, he thought.

Ever since he could remember, his father had set tests for him and Rafe. To teach them, his mother said, to prepare them for the world he thought was waiting for them; but Seth doubted that his father, orphaned at nine by a boating accident in Narragansett Bay and taken in by the Sisters of Saint Joseph, had any blueprint for the raising of his sons. Do a hundred pushups without stopping; swim the length of Nonesuch Pond, in the dark, in winter. He taught them to shoot—both boys could handle his beloved war-souvenir Luger, a Winchester, and a Daisy by the time they were ten—and not to hesitate, or not where he could see it. Raphael took the tests seriously. (The time they were supposed to fire the Daisy between the bars of the cockatiel's cage at a target on the big scarlet oak out back, and Rafe had hit the bird.) Seth, with his brother to walk point for him, figured out a better way. Often their father would forget, once a little time had passed, or have a change of heart and rescind the challenge. Seth learned to wait.

The fresh-cut logs, their smell sharp as vinegar, dropped onto the stack with neat little knocking sounds. They worked as they always worked together, in silence. The kind of silence into which Louisa would have flung Dear Nonsense, like a lifeline; the kind of silence in which his father came home from Mercy Hospital, where he was a surgical nurse, smelling of ether (which always made Seth think of lilacs) and the brown, tangy odor of blood. At first Seth just kept pace with his father, who trudged doggedly back and forth, now and then glancing up at the house. It hadn't turned out quite right—from this angle the corner nearest the driveway was clearly lower than the other—and he couldn't let go of it. That one corner absorbed more of his attention than the rest of the house put together. The way, since the business a year ago, Rafe seemed to blot up all his fathering. (A Suicidal Gesture, Dr. Armijo, the shrink, had called Rafe's taking of not quite enough Valium; didn't that mean, not the real thing?) One August night, months after his brother had come home from the hospital, Seth, sitting on the dark screened porch, had watched his father walk into the living room and put a hand on Rafe's shoulder. His voice came clearly in the humid air. *You're my boy.*

Seth stopped to pull off his sweatshirt. The warm, un-November air felt creepy on his bare chest. Walking back and forth, he watched the fog shrink slowly into the woods, unraveling around the ghostlike trunks of the birches. He speeded up. One more log per armload; two. When he'd started at Saint Jude's the year before, he'd gone out for JV football; now he could bench 160 pounds, curl 100. In the shower he traced the gleaming arcs of his pecs and lats under the hot pouring water. Some days he felt a kind of humming all over, a current that ran through his muscles like a continuous charge.

The sea of logs was going down fast; patches of bright green moss shone in the gaps. Seth could hear his father breathing, *ha, a-ha,* each time they passed each other.

He'd watched Rafe trying, this last year, not to be their father. Majoring in philosophy; and his girls—there were always girls— somehow reinforced that side of him, the mystical side (misty, musty, mush, their father said). Seth could have told Rafe that running away from a thing still meant it determined your direction. Sometimes he felt that his life had been owned before he got it: Rafe had the experiences, but they passed through him like sunlight through a prism, leaving Seth to see what they meant.

Forget Rafe, he thought; you can win this sucker. He tried the trick that Rafe had taught him, the one he'd learned from the shrink: look around you, focus on what's real. Say to yourself, *I see a chair, I see a meal-tray, I see a green cinderblock wall.* A single raven, swinging high in one of the maples, sent its terse wintry sound into the too warm air. I see red berries on the fire thorn, Seth told himself, trotting over the stony ground. I see deadwood tied in bundles. I see a stone wall.

The loose logs were down to a scattering. He finished them off in three armloads to his father's one, and said triumphantly, "I win."

Francis Godburn said, "Wait a minute. Just hold your horses."

Seth rubbed his hands, pulled his elbows back to stretch his cramped shoulders. His father walked slowly from one end of the long stack, now as high as his head, to the other. "Nope," he said finally. One by one he poked a finger into several chinks on Seth's side. "Look at that. Look at that. That." He thrust his whole hand into one crevice. "Job's got to be done right, not just done." He waved the other arm in the direction of his own side. The tight-packed logs, neat as hospital corners, offered no invitation to copperheads or skinks.

Seth picked up his sweatshirt and shook off the pine needles. He wiped his face and neck with slow, deliberate motions that said how little he cared. The thing was, they got so they waited for the tests, he and Rafe. Looked forward to them—to being pulled out of themselves into something else, something that took you over; to the sweet relief of not having to choose.

"November's November." His father's voice was rough with the kindness that came after a test. "Better put your shirt on."

It wasn't the girl's skin but her hair that was the startling thing.

They were sitting, the five of them, at the kitchen table, having what Louisa called tideover food—apples and cheese and homemade cracked wheat bread, tea that tasted like oranges. Seth put his hand to his own head. There were furrows across his scalp, and the back flattened with dismaying abruptness where it met his neck. Shaved, it would be ugly. The girl's skull, covered with no more than a quarter-inch of black hair, was perfect, shining, red-brown. She sat in silence across the table beside Raphael, in a turquoise T-shirt and a dozen silver bracelets that slid musically up and down her thin forearms.

Girls, Seth thought for the second time that day, always girls, and damned if he knew why. His brother's hair stood out all around his head with the frail radiance of a dandelion gone to seed. How had he gotten his flat, tea-colored hair to do that? Seth looked from one head to the other, Rafe's to the girl's. If his brother's last year at Saint Jude's was anything to go by, they were getting it on.

Raphael had greeted Hugo first, dropping down on one knee in the gravel and pulling the ecstatic dog into his arms. The girl, in a red woollen hat and a pea jacket, stood beside him with her arms crossed and her hands tucked into her sleeves like a nun. When Raphael rose, Louisa hugged him, head against his chest, listening surreptitiously to his heart. He had on a lavender wool scarf and a black broad-brimmed hat that Seth had never seen before. "From up there I couldn't tell if you're a rabbi or a cowboy," Francis Godburn said. He shook

Raphael's hand, then the girl's. Hanging back on the porch, their father had had time to compose his face; even so, Seth could make out satisfaction in Rafe's eyes. Let him get past *this*, the eyes had said.

Now Francis Godburn asked questions about college from a list he seemed to have prepared in advance, and Raphael, listing slightly toward the girl so that their arms almost touched, answered in a voice that made it clear there was more to be said. At the foot of the table Louisa had picked up a square of cream-colored linen in a silver hoop and was pecking at it with a needle; she looked up watchfully every few pecks. The girl drank from a white china mug. Her eyes took in the kitchen—the long double-glazed windows, the open shelves Francis Godburn had built of clear pine, the counters piled with shiny blue balloons, the picture of the Sacred Heart in the corner by the back door—but Seth had the feeling it was them she was recording, like an anthropologist encountering a strange tribe.

"Theology?" Francis Godburn said. "Theology? What kind of a subject is that? A man gets enough of that at Mass on Sunday, seems to me." But his voice was less hectoring than usual. Seth thought he was probably still in shock because of the girl, at whom he carefully did not look.

"It's a perfectly good subject, Pop." Their father hated to be called Pop. "A four-credit course. In which I happen to have an A average so far. Want some jam to go on that?" he asked the girl. She shook her head and smiled at him, a quick sidelong flash of a smile.

"Theology. Sociology. Mother of God. Might's well join the Peace Corps and be done with it."

Seth tried unsuccessfully to catch his brother's eye. Raphael drank tea with his little finger crooked away from the handle of his mug in a way sure to strike their father as sissy. His wrist looked as fragile as the girl's; but the gesture, provocative, was one he would not have dared before he went away.

"That one, I admire it very very much," the girl said shyly to Louisa. She was looking at the antique saw that Louisa had fastened, teeth up, on the lintel above the back door. Louisa nodded encouragingly.

"At home sometime they put shark jaw like that. You know? The big one." The girl's long, thin arms stretched wide to illustrate. Home was Kenya. She was an exchange student from a small Methodist college in Nairobi. Her name was really Ngozi, Ngozi Lucille, but here everyone called her Lucy, like Raphael, it was easier. Now that she'd found it, her voice bubbled faintly like water through pipes; Francis Godburn, not quite looking at her, turned one ear in her direction as if listening for a fault in the plumbing.

Under the table Hugo groaned. Lucy bent down to rub his nose. Seth saw his father look at the cropped black hair like coarse cotton thread, every strand distinct; at the long bare neck with its scattering of little fleshy moles in the shape of a rough letter C. They made Seth think of a rhyme Louisa used to recite.

> Mole on the face, suffers disgrace;
> Mole on the neck, trouble by the peck.

Lucy said softly, "At home, the old ones, they say why do dogs have a cold nose? Because they were coming very very late to the Ark. And like that, they had to sit next to the rail." It wasn't clear whether this was addressed to all of them or meant only for Hugo's ears.

The morning's fat fly skimmed the table, barely missing the butter dish. Francis Godburn pushed back his chair and stood up. "Well, long as you're holed up in the Berkshires you won't get drafted. That's one thing." He opened the cellar door. They heard his boots on the wooden steps.

Louisa held up a shimmering length of scarlet floss and began trying to thread her needle. "I remember the day the war ended," she said. "Our whole village hung on the rope of the First Baptist bell, one by one. All two hundred of us. It tolled the whole afternoon. Six months after that, to the day, I met Mr. Godburn. He was just back from Okinawa."

"This one ain't our war, Lou." Francis Godburn reappeared, carrying a fly swatter. "They don't need any sons of ours." One hand rested on his wife's shoulder; the swatter slapped the oak table by Seth's elbow. "Got him!" But he was wrong.

Seth stared at his brother, willing their eyes to meet in the old way; but Rafe was looking from their father to Lucy and back again. His arm shifted in a way that meant he'd reached for Lucy's hand under the table.

Lucy raised her head. "At home we say, the flies, they may dine at the King's table. Because the flies, you know, the flies on Christ body, they look like nails. And like that, they stop the soldiers to drive more nails in."

The fly lighted on the table inches from Francis Godburn. Lucy smiled up at him. Arm raised, he hesitated. Then he laid the fly swatter on the counter and sat down. Raphael turned his head away, but not before Seth had read on his brother's face the quick, sharp disappointment.

Seth had been sure that Rafe would make time for him. He'd imagined them driving down to the creek in the old flesh-colored Delta-88 Rafe had bought for a hundred bucks the year before. The car, with its worn upholstery like moleskin and its smell of old sneakers and the moat of fog all around it, would have the close, safe feeling of the confessional. Rafe would tell him things.

Instead, when Louisa took Lucy upstairs to unpack (Francis Godburn having underlined, by a good deal of throat-clearing and arm-folding, the fact that she and Raphael were separated by the length of the corridor), Rafe went out to the car alone. Seth followed as far as the back porch, waiting to be asked. His father came out and sat down on the stoop. He began cleaning the Luger with an old undershirt.

"Hey! Rafe!" Seth shouted.

When he got to the car, his brother was looking in the rear-view mirror and flicking at his hair with a tortoise-shell pic. Seth slapped the window. Raphael rolled it down two or three inches. It was like when they were kids—begging to tag along. Seth put one hand on the glass that separated them. "You going to the creek?"

Raphael hesitated, looked, finally, straight at Seth.

"Lucy's neat," Seth said. His voice came out louder than he meant, and he realized as he spoke that this was the absolutely wrong thing to say, but he plunged on. "They like her."

Raphael said, "I gotta be by myself for a while. You can dig it, right, Mops?"

The childhood nickname made Seth mute. He took a step back, his hand still curled over the top of the window. A smile deepened the long dimple by Rafe's mouth, *I know something you don't*, like when they were kids and each got a box of Raisinets and Rafe ate his all at once but Seth saved his in a drawer under his folded jockey shorts, where Rafe stole them one by one. When Seth finally caught him, they'd go for each other. Their father, approving, let them work it out. *A boy don't fight his brother, he's never going to love him.*

Raphael turned the key in the ignition. The engine whirred and stumbled, then caught. Seth let go of the window. For a second Raphael sat listening to the rough rhythm of the pistons. Then his shoulder thrust forward and the Olds took off in a spray of gravel.

Seth yanked open the back door. His father said, "Rhode Island's too small for him now," his voice oddly gentle as he pulled out the Luger's bolt.

"We need to dance," Louisa announced after dinner, an hour and a half of bumpy conversation and sudden silences during which they'd all eaten more than they wanted. She stood by the front door in her red caftan sorting through old 45s, picking out the ones with "blue" in the title. "I'll play you" (a little bow toward Lucy) "the songs of my youth, shall I?"

Seth carried armloads of seasoned oak and his father laid a neat fire in the fireplace, wasteful as it was (he pointed out to Louisa) when an open flue sucked good electrically heated air out of the house. Raphael and Lucy pushed the sofa and chairs against the walls. At Louisa's insistence they all rubbed balloons on their heads and stuck them to the ceiling. Seth was detailed to blow up the balloons his mother hadn't gotten around to. Exhaling, he watched smooth blue skin glide back and forth across Lucy's skull. His brother hadn't given any sign that he remembered the balloons of 1965 or even wondered about the balloons of now. Louisa threw a linen cloth over the coffee table and set out red wine and long-stemmed fragile glasses and the rest of the chocolate pecan pie. Now and then someone tripped over Hugo, who patrolled the room in faltering slow motion.

The room, the people in it, were transformed. The long windows, filled with moonless night, were a dark liquid in which reflected lamplight and firelight shone. At the north end of the room, where the floor sloped down to the one unfortunate corner, Seth's face swam towards him. Behind him Lucy, dimmer than the others with their abrupt white hands and faces, moved slowly around the edges of the room. She picked up a framed photograph from a table, looked at it, put it down. Turning, Seth watched her go to Raphael, who had crouched down to lay another log on the fire. She knelt beside him with her bare knees on the slate hearth, and the fire, blazing up, outlined her with light. She wore a sleeveless yellow dress and a jagged necklace of silver and ivory; her bare brown shoulders tilted forward. Seth felt the way he did when he was out running on their narrow dirt road at night. His good madras shirt tightened like a bandage across his chest.

> 's awf'ly nice—
> 's Paradise—
> 's what I long—to—see

The old turntable hesitated, wavered, then picked up speed. Raphael pulled Lucy to her feet and they began to dance. Francis Godburn sat in an overstuffed chair against the wall, gripping the arms like someone in an airplane for the first time. Louisa walked over to him and stood holding out her hand until he got up to lead her back and forth across the floor in a series of neat-cornered boxes. Seth stared past the dancing couples into the fire. Sparks clung briefly to the chimney back, winked, and went out. Flying geese, his mother called them.

"Fools Rush In." "Am I Blue." "Gandy Dancers' Ball." Lucy's yellow skirt floated out around her burnished knees. Between dances she drank red wine, gulping thirstily. She and Raphael jitterbugged. Seth could see the hair under her arms, a patch of darker brown. He thought how it would smell, would taste. He laid his tongue against the shoulder of his sweater. Outside the wind began to pick up, rattling the bare branches of the maples and tossing spirals of dead leaves against the windows. Louisa danced with Seth. He held her clumsily, his muscles no use for this, and tried to imitate his father's boxes. Over her shoulder, he could see his father watching, see Rafe turn Lucy so that his own back hid her from their father's view.

"Blue Moon." "Someone to Watch over Me."

Lucy asked Seth to dance. She danced with her head tucked to one side, teetering a little from the wine. The cluster of moles on her neck glistened, and there was a fleck of yellow lint caught in her eyelashes. Seth could smell her faint lemon smell and the wine on her breath and his own nervous sourness. He held her well away from him—it made the boxes easier—and kept swallowing. Her eyes were on a level with his throat. "The apple, it stick in Adam throat when he is taking it from Eve. And God say, okay, it is there for always." Her smile was slow, dreamy, not anxious the way it had been that afternoon. A balloon detached itself from the ceiling and drifted down.

When Rafe came to claim Lucy, Seth poured wine, which he was not allowed to have, into one of the fragile glasses, then went over and rubbed the stray balloon across his head and stuck it back up. The wine tasted dark and heavy, the way it looked. Louisa came and sat down on the sofa next to Seth, fanning herself. He wedged his wineglass behind a cushion, out of sight.

Raphael gave Lucy's waist a squeeze and left the room. She danced on by herself in the middle of the shining floor, eyes nearly closed, one hand clasping her own bare shoulder. Her long fingers tapped the back of her neck. Her necklace caught the light, shining like long silver teeth. Another balloon floated to the floor.

After a few minutes Francis Godburn set down his wineglass and walked over to Lucy. Slowly he moved one foot forward, then back. He shifted to the other foot: forward, back. He picked each foot up and set it down with awkward tentativeness, as if it had fallen asleep. One hand gripped the knot of his necktie.

> Ain't misbehavin'
> I'm savin' my love
> For you

A foot apart, the two bodies, one bulky and wide-chested in its stiff white shirt, the other slender and pliant, began to move in a rocky approximation of the same rhythm.

"That's dancing fish," Louisa said, leaning toward Seth and speaking into his left ear. "That's what we used to call it, when you dance without touching."

Seth, watching them, saw in his father a sudden, wholly unsuspected sweetness. It brushed his face for an instant, then flashed away: the sweetness of someone learning. His stumbling movements slowly, humbly fitted themselves to the girl's. The firelight smoothed his face into almost-Rafe's, softened the long dimple into a crescent of tender shadow.

Raphael stopped still in the doorway. Seeing him, Louisa patted the seat next to her on the sofa, but he gave a curt shake of his head.

Lucy, dancing with her back to the door, didn't see him; but Francis Godburn turned his head toward his son. The angle of it offered a silent challenge, his eyes on Raphael while his body went on with its rough translation of Lucy's.

Raphael began to walk slowly around the edges of the room. Something in his step, hesitant, bated, told Seth what he was thinking. *I see a chair. I see a table.* Wind shook the long windows.

Do something, Seth thought. Rain began, fat distinct drops that hit the windows with the force of hail. No one else seemed to hear it. Helen Morgan's creamy voice praised Loch Lomond. Louisa, on the sofa, swayed in time to the music, eyes closed, stockinged foot patting the floor. A balloon drifted down, then another. Lucy, dancing, laid one hand against the side of her neck. The shape of her head seemed naked, intimate. Confused, Seth felt the movement of the dancing in his own body, tapping out the wordless message that he, Seth, was no different. He would take her, too, if he could. He looked at his brother's rigid back.

Do something.

But Rafe only stood there, as though he had to make absolutely sure of something, while more and more balloons descended. Their motion mimicked the movements of the dancers, dreamy and purposeless. One after another they drifted down, a slow, slow storm of blue.

Rain came in earnest in the night, with unseasonable thunder and cracks of lightning. Seth heard his brother's door close sharply, his brother's feet slapping down the hall to the guest room, the clap of another door closing. All at dream-slow speed, the sounds dilating like echoes in a cave.

Sliding back into sleep, Seth thought, If I can hear, they can, too.

Years later he could still see every detail of the early morning living room. How the first light through the long windows, wet with last night's rain, gilded the edges of things, turning the familiar strange. How they sat, his father and his mother (the girl was asleep upstairs), without moving. The furniture pushed back against the walls made the room look like a doctor's waiting room. Louisa sat where she had the night before, on the sofa. Her hands lay in her lap with the palms curved upward. Francis Godburn sat across the room in an old ladder-back rocker, but he was not rocking. He sat upright, his back not touching the chair's. Seth had to shuffle through blue balloons to reach the sofa.

What he could never remember afterwards was how they told him, what they said. Instantly, it seemed, he understood. Rafe had slept with the girl openly—noisily—under his parents' roof; Rafe had been sent out to the woods with Hugo and his father's Luger. Time Hugo's misery ended, they all knew that, said his father's face; his mother's face told him that this time she had not interfered.

The room smelled of rain-washed earth and clean, chill air. The three of them waited in silence, eyes on the painful ribbon of light where the front door had not quite closed. Seth could hear the ticking of the baseboard heaters. One bare foot began to tap the cold floor; he curled his toes under, to stop it. He remembered reading some-where that the faster your heart beats, the slower time moves. His heart was ticking faster than the baseboard heaters. Slowly, invisibly, he flexed his quads, his pecs, *one one thousand, two one thousand*. He thought, The heart is a muscle.

Outside there was a single gunshot, a small flat sound. Louisa flinched. Francis Godburn sat staring at the stretch of polished floor between his feet. His face looked caved-in, old. Already, Seth knew, he was regretting the challenge—would have taken it back or let it slide.

Why didn't Rafe wait? Seth thought. Just fucking *wait* five minutes?

Finally there was a sound at the door. Seth's heart bumped, re-started. Slowly the door swung open. Seth could see the dark-green rhododendron by the front step, a strip of sky stained rose. Hugo stepped slowly over the threshold.

The room seemed to narrow and grow dark. Seth could barely make out his father, frozen in place with his head turned toward the empty doorway. Last night's rain dripped from the rhododendron. The first slanting rays of sunlight polished every pointed leaf, shined it into a tree of silver knives. His mother's hands flew up; one reached for Seth. For no more than an instant, a half-heartbeat (but he thought it): Now I'm their boy. Then horror filled him. He grabbed his mother's hand and squeezed it, hard. *I see a chair. I see a fireplace.* Hugo shambled into the center of the room and lay down with his head on his paws.

And then the doorway filled with clean-washed light; light caught in Rafe's absurd aureole of hair as if the sun, finally freeing itself from the horizon, had flung him there. The room was suddenly full of the sound of breathing. His brother stood straight in the doorway, shoulders back. His face wore an expression Seth knew well, the one they had so often seen on their father's, the one that said, *This is a test.*

Salvage

1

"Dzień dobry, dzień dobry, dzień dobry."

They are like figures in an old-fashioned dance, a vaudeville routine translated. He, tall and lanky and professorially stoop-shouldered; she, short and broad. He stands in the hall in late afternoon sunlight while she circles him as if he were a maypole. "Pan Professor," she cries, taking his jacket, his briefcase. "All—ready. When you eat, tell. What you wish for?"

Sometimes Stephen wishes for an English-to-English interpreter. He finds himself talking to Pani Pentowska in macaronic sentences, drawing heavily on the little Polish he heard as a child, huddled with his grandmother when his mother was out of earshot. "Good," he says. "*Dobrze.*"

She throws back her head to look up at him. "Good. Yes? *Bardzo* good."

She takes a string bag from the big mahogany wardrobe and shows him the ham she bought that morning, in a red-and-white can printed in English, "Krakus Export—Product of Poland." At Polno Market, Fat Marya had pulled it out from under her black tent of a coat. It will be good with slices of apple and a honey glaze, she conveys to him. For next time; not today.

In the living room Stephen pours himself a shot of vodka from a bottle in which a spear of buffalo grass floats upright. The vodka explodes softly in his empty stomach. He sits down on the sofa with the bottle beside him and sips the second glass, skirting the empty space in his mind, listening to the clang and tinkle coming from the kitchen, where Pani Pentowska chops leeks and onions and kielbasa.

"You eat," says Pani Pentowska from the doorway. Coming into the room, she makes a quick pass over table tops and shelves, rolling up bits of string, smoothing and folding brown wrapping paper as if it were linen. "Bad," she says, waving her hand. "*Bardzo* bad." At first he thinks she means the mess; but she motions to him to come to the windows.

On the wide marble sills the plants have turned toward the light. The smaller ones have a dusty rented look. The asparagus fern has sprinkled the wooden floor with dry brown needles. Pani Pentowska pinches yellowed leaves off the devil's ivy one by one, counting *raz dwa trzy cztery*, and shoves them into her apron pocket. Close up, she smells like Brussels sprouts. Her barbed hair, grey mixed with an improbable reddish brown, sticks out around her ears.

"Water. They need." Her stubby fingers make motions like rain falling. "Pan Professor, you fix?"

He answers as quickly as if it were Rachel asking him. "Okay," he says, to his own surprise.

"*Dobrze.*" She begins picking plant lice off a schefflera, examining each tiny caramel shell tenderly before she crushes it between her fingers.

2

After Pani Pentowska has served dinner and gone, Stephen checks over the space around the windows. In the tiny courtyard two stories below, a street-lamp blinks on, wavers for a moment, then steadies. The courtyard is empty except for a small man with thinning grey hair pushing a child—his granddaughter?—on a swing. The little girl, in a plaid coat and white knee socks, looks about four years old, the same age as Stephen's daughter, Nora. Stephen pulls open the French doors and leans out over the tiny balcony. In the surprisingly warm October air, the voices of the old man and the child come clearly. *"Jeszcze, czy już?"* he asks her. *"Jeszcze, czy już?"* More? Or enough?

Nora loves swings; she will love this narrow grey courtyard with its single birch tree when she comes. If, he corrects himself. Rachel, reluctant in the first place to bring Nora to Eastern Europe (she thinks of the Iron Curtain as a solid structure studded with spikes, like an iron maiden), keeps finding reasons to delay. She knows the numbers. Three and a half million Jews in Poland before the war; afterward, seven thousand.

Stephen turns away, snaps on the radio. While the Voice of America flings shards of news at him in Special English, he sits on the sofa in the growing dark, in the land of his ancestors. He thinks that Rachel is right. He is a romantic and a fool. It has been a mistake to come here; a mistake to think these people would have anything to say to him, or he to them; a mistake to imagine, in his vague professorial way, that the lives of past generations could be salvaged. The Poles have always been hostile to outsiders.

3

In her one-room flat, Pani Pentowska pulls the curtains across the night sky, shutting out the grey light from Marszalkowska Street. She unpacks her string bag, puts the sack of onions into the cupboard over the little refrigerator, the bottle of milk inside. She'll have to drink it by noontime tomorrow or it will spoil. On the rack beside it she sets the chunk of ham that the Pan Professor will never miss.

Next to the bed is a wooden table with a small lamp. The chair in front of it is covered with one of the sheepskins Jerzy cured in the years before he died. It is worn now in places. She turns on the lamp and sits down to write her nightly letter to her husband.

Jerzy mój. My Monday-Wednesday-Friday buys dollars now. These Fulbrighters are much better to work for than the Embassy people. Though they are like happy, baffled children, she thinks. *I give him a good rate, one hundred to the dollar.* She takes the dollars to the Narodowy Bank where they lie in neat stacks in the vault. With dollars she bought their daughter, Bożena, an apartment when she married her good-for-nothing student. *But now, who knows. Solidarność! Milk and vodka, meat and even cheese disappearing from the stores. Nie ma is all you hear—none of this, none of that. Soon it will take dollars for even the simplest things. In the Old Town yesterday, by the statue of Sigismund, I heard a man offer one hundred twenty.*

It is cold in the flat. The ink has clotted. She shakes the pen like a thermometer, snapping her wrist. A blue-black drop flies out onto the wooden table top, and she wipes it away with her finger.

Today was warm for October, as warm as the autumn you came back. Your face with its deep scar like a seam down the side, still red then, your souvenir of the Eastern Front.

She thinks of the year just after the war, in the big attic under the rafters. She held the brush in her hand, and Bożena's thick, autumn-colored hair sifted through her fingers, parting above the flat white collar of her school uniform to show the violet birthmark at the nape of her neck, shaped like a bird's wing. Jerzy's face is overlaid now by her own face in the mirror day after day. The past itself is overlaid by all the days between then and now; it is fixed like a fossil, deeper than knowledge or forgiveness, without smell or sound or color. *There is no one any more who calls me by my name.* She is called by her functions: Mama, Pani.

The pen scratches across the rough wheat-colored paper. She crosses out the last sentence.

4

Holding out his *legitymacja* with the plastic-coated photograph, Stephen approaches the kiosk. Inside sits the same woman who is always there. She is middle-aged and has dyed-black hair held flat to her temples by a hairnet. She shakes her head. She points to a white banner the size of two or three bedsheets, with large dark letters that spell out "*STRAJK*," stretched across the massive iron gates.

"*Proszę*—" he begins, *please*, intending to ask what's going on, when classes will meet again; but she keeps on shaking her head. He turns away.

Students cluster thickly around a platform on the other side of the gates, milling around and shouting. Coatless despite the cold, several are wearing T-shirts with "*Solidarność*" across the front in red. On the platform one of his students, Urszula of the dark-red hair, is swiftly handing out fliers. As she turns her head from side to side, her fat braid snaps out and curls back on her shoulder like some glossy animal. The best student in Stephen's American literature class, she is quick and daring, willing to take risks with her English. I am Jewish, she told him a few weeks ago, watching his face. They stood in the corridor smoking during the break, down at the end by the high barred window, a little apart from the others. She said, We have nothing to lose. On the dirty green wall behind her someone had chalked a swastika and the Russian hammer-and-sickle, with an "equals" sign between them.

On the platform beside Urszula, in identical carefully faded American jeans, her boyfriend Jacek climbs onto a stool and begins to speak. He gestures and his eyes are bright. How the German tanks rolled toward Kudno in the autumn of 1939; how the Polish cavalry charged them with horses and swords. The page of notes he holds, Stephen sees, is embellished on the back with the same motifs as the notes he takes in class—fleshy arrows and zigzag bolts of lightning, bold and compact as tattoos. Jacek doesn't need to consult it. He spins off consonants into the crowd, and the air around the platform glitters. Seeing no way to get past the hairnetted Cerberus, Stephen stands like a child with his hands curled around the cold iron gates, and watches.

5

Two in the morning. Rain sounds as if it were being flung against the windows in handfuls. Down Miodowa Street the klaxon of an ambulance repeats its two-note bleating call, which Stephen always hears as *"Nie ma, nie ma."* The empty space alongside his body in the bed is almost solid, like the cold length of a mummy.

The living room of the house in Nebraska prints itself on the back of his closed eyelids. Set into the side of a rare hill, not far east of Hogback Mountain, it is small, compact, two stories of silver weathered boards and tall windows, ringed with pines and green-black spruces that look as if they'd been varnished. Stephen built it himself. It took two years. It is built completely out of salvaged materials: hand-hewn six-by-sixes from an abandoned farmhouse; wide cedar barn-boards; casement windows from the old Stockman's Bank in town. Rachel nailed the mezuzah she'd had since college onto the orange-painted doorframe, making the joke she made whenever they moved, that really she should only put up half of it since only one of them was Jewish. From the front porch they could see one end of tiny Bitter Lake. The air was so clear it threw your voice back against your teeth.

He gets up. On the kitchen walls (against the rules of his landlady, Pani Wierzbicka—toothy old aristocrat) he has taped several opera posters from the Teatr Wielki. He sits at the kitchen table, where a contorted pink-and-blue Othello sneers down at him, and begins drafting. A network of pipes suspended from the ceiling in front of the living room windows, as intricate as the embroidery on old Wierzbicka's sofa cushions; and the whole thing will have to connect with the water source in the bathroom. On the back of one of Pani Pentowska's pieces of brown wrapping paper, he makes a list. Pipe: two hundred feet, at least. Valves, washers, slip nuts, set screws. He starts a new column headed "Tools." Duck-billed pliers, open-end wrench (and a Stillson, too, if he can find one), hacksaw, pipe threader. He remembers the mist rising off Bitter Lake in the still, bright dawn.

6

At Polno Market the long tables are draped with sheets or blankets, some with newspapers taped together; there are narrow aisles between them, and the whole thing is sheltered by huge awnings. She goes first, to show the Pan Professor the way.

Just inside the entrance is a man in an overcoat muttering, *"Cielę-czyna, cielęczyna."* He is holding a large black gladstone bag, the kind doctors carry. As they pass, he takes out a bundle and lifts a corner of the white gauze wrapping, like a mother offering a glimpse of her baby's face. The lump of meat inside is fleshy, pale, marbled with pink blood. "Veal," Pani Pentowska tells the Pan Professor. They're slaughtering the young cattle now because there will be no feed for them this winter.

The word *Amerykanin* and the Pan Professor's dollars work wonders. From under the blankets and newspapers come lumpy bits of metal in odd shapes, and tools like Jerzy used to have. What they need, they find. Some of it they'll have to come back for tomorrow or the next day.

They take the trolley back to the Third of May Street. There are a dozen flower-sellers in the cavelike space under the bridge. The colors spread out against the dank grey stone are like a fire on a dark night.

"It's a treasure hunt," says the Pan Professor as they climb the stairs, clanking. She can see that he wants to explain what a treasure hunt is. She doesn't tell him that her Tuesday-Thursday, a professor of history from the city of New York, gives birthday parties for his three daughters, and each time they have a treasure hunt. What she and the Pan Professor are doing is not at all like that. Americans are children.

7

The spigot is a problem, and the longer pipe. But Pani Pentowska has connections. One day Stephen wakes to find a small thicket of pipes bristling in the hallway.

In the afternoons, while dinner is cooking, she works alongside him, handing him pieces of pipe and valves and wrenches. He points to what he needs and she names it in Polish. He practices the names silently, the consonants clutching at his tongue. At close range, her Brussels-sprouts smell makes him think of how people in the Middle Ages wore garlic around their necks to ward off disease. The odor begins to seem inevitable, familiar, like the cool heft of pipe corners in his palm, the groan of the wrench against metal threads.

While they work she tells him stories of her past, in English that is somehow miraculously improved. Her voice has a detached quality, as if the stories are ones she has told so often that by now they seem to be about someone else. But Stephen listens, and after a while he sees the firelit faces of the men and women in the Resistance; the icy crossing of the Vistula; the years of waiting for those who vanished into the swell of nameless dead.

His loneliness lessens. He begins to accept the fact that Rachel and Nora are not coming. Perhaps, he thinks, he was wrong about the Poles; perhaps it is possible to understand. To know a real person in this godforsaken place. He wonders what her name is. Katrzyna? Małgorzata? To ask her, would he use the polite pronoun, or the familiar? The familiar is for friendship; but it's also what a master might use to a servant.

8

Jerzy mój. She chews the end of her pen, shuffles her feet in their felt house slippers. The room is cold. Pushing up the sleeves of her robe, she rubs her palms along the inside of her arms. The soft skin catches on her calluses. She gets up. In the collection of cardboard boxes piled on top of the wardrobe, she finds Jerzy's dark-red wool scarf and wraps it around her neck. She pads to the kitchen end of the room and turns on the gas flame under the teakettle. From the wooden cupboard she takes out a thin china cup and saucer painted with roses and winding green vines. The tea is hot and sweet. She sits down again and picks up her pen.

Today we connected the pipes. They hang from the ceiling with brackets he made from coathangers.

Americans' problems always seem to be mechanical problems. Cars that won't start, doors that won't close, trains that fail to arrive on time. What do they know about the things that come down from outside like a giant's hand, grinding flesh and bone? About countries built on layer after mealy layer of such things?

Tomorrow we try it out for the first time. If things were different—if Americans were different—I could make a special meal, lay the ivory linen cloth. Chicken roasted with apples and plums; soup; a bowl of fat mushrooms. I would take off my apron and stand beside the table in my black dress with the lace at the neck. Light the candles in the center, and the glasses with their long stems would shine.

She imagines how, after the meal, they would go into the living room and the Pan Professor would turn the handle. Water would sift through the air. The green leaves of the plants, heart-shaped and star-shaped, would curl toward the mist, breathing out a loamy smell. Light would glint off the Pan Professor's white teeth when he smiled and called her by name.

If things were not as they are.

Laying down her pen, she gets up slowly and goes to the window. The dark glass gives back a vague ghost-figure, square in a pale robe, eyes white-rimmed holes. She puts out her hand. Slowly her bunched fingertips touch the blurred mouth. She says the word she hasn't heard for years.

"Anna," she says.

9

Jak sie Pani nazywa, Stephen practices in the morning before Pani Pentowska comes. He has decided on the polite form, softened by a warm voice, a smile.

But she is cool and businesslike. She keeps her blue-striped apron tied over her dress; its pockets sag with wrenches, pliers, valves. When he asks for what he needs, she slaps it into his palm like a surgical nurse.

At last he twists the red rubber-coated handle. There is a pause; then a fine mist begins to fall. He turns to her, smiles, starts to speak. But she says only, "*Już* finish."

Someone Else

Mary Rose Klossner fell in love with my husband when she was eleven months old. We stood in my kitchen doorway, thirteen years ago this fall, the four of us: Mary Rose and her father and Loren and me. Early evening: the last of the sun, slanting in through the open door, cut right across us.

"We just, I don't know. We run out of just about everything again," Will Klossner said. He squinted against the light, and his dirty-blonde hair fell across his forehead in clumps. More and more, since Ella Klossner died, he looked like a caricature of a midwestern farmer. Standing there angled like a coathanger, too tall for the door-frame, in worn jeans and a plaid flannel shirt missing a button.

Mary Rose was a long baby, held in Will Klossner's arms, long legs dangling down. Her feet were bare; that came of having no mother to dress her. But it was warm still, Indian summer.

"We've got plenty," I said. "Whatever you need."

He gave me a confused look. "Have you had dinner?" I asked. He shook his head. "Well, then. Let's see. We've already eaten, finished up a roast right down to the bone, no leftovers even. How about eggs?"

Loren was paying no attention to any of this. He wasn't very good at practical matters because they didn't interest him much, or maybe it went the other way around. He left things like this—the what to do with what, how to get from here to there stuff—to me. He stood in the shaft of late sun, looking at the baby.

Not a beautiful child. You first felt rather than saw her; then, caught by that mysterious pull, you looked again. She had eyes that were luminous and almost without color. I saw them grow larger, saw her gaze catch in Loren's ruddy beard, which glittered in the light. He is tall and square-shouldered and reddish all over—he comes from good Swedish stock on both sides. The lines raying out around Loren's eyes deepened with his smile, which seemed to spread into the corners of the room. The child's eyes in that long moment gleamed like opals. Behind them you'd have sworn she was thinking, evaluating things, was—*amused*. And behind the amusement lay, even then, some kind of question. I had the strongest urge to move suddenly, to snap the thread that spun itself between my husband and this child.

Then she broke it with a deep, throaty chuckle—the baby. I watched her hands, surprisingly large, open and close, open and close.

"I'll get the eggs," I said. My words tumbled out fast. "Milk, butter," talking a list, "Rice Krispies for tomorrow morning." I got busy, finding a grocery bag and shaking it open, filling it with things they'd need. On top I put a banana to slice over the cereal.

Twelve—almost thirteen—years later, standing at the edge of Elbow Lake in the fizzy April air, I ask myself a question. Were we happy then? Across the lake, the densely wooded bluff is a rough weave of browns, threaded now with red-tinged new green and the bitter yellow of the willows. Sun strikes off the trunks of the birches, and here and there a house gleams through a chink in the trees. Happy. I thought we were, at the time. Isn't that as good as? Isn't it as close as you *come* in life?

Maybe *happy* is too wide a word. It's a little Minnesota town; life here isn't exciting. Content, then. We were content, at ease with each other and with the life we had. Oh, there were times—those lopped-off, midwinter, lightless fights—when Loren would go out ice fishing and I would wish he'd fall into the hole and the water, black as oil, would close over his head, pull him far out under the ice and never let go. Once I threw all his things out into the driveway. I didn't bother with suitcases or boxes. They lay there on the gravel in the cold afternoon light: clothes and shoes and boots, a thunder of odd dark shapes; fishing rods snagging the air; his tools from the shed. I didn't stop to think how, if anyone came by and saw all that, it made me look more of a fool than him. In the morning, everything was gone. Loren had gone out in the middle of the night and brought it all in and put it away, stowing each thing where it belonged. He didn't say a word. Everything was the same as before. That was early on; I never lost control of myself like that again.

We got set in our ways somewhat, I guess, what with not having children. Not that we didn't try, at least the first six years. But when Dr. Sorensen told us for sure that we couldn't—*I* couldn't—the desire just gradually drained away. The act didn't seem natural anymore. Like fish, all that flopping and slapping, wet, cold. Something you only do in the deep of night, under the quilts, and your arms and legs so tangled up with someone else's that you can hardly tell them apart.

Loren was a thoughtful man, he saw how I felt. "Irene," he said one night, the two of us lying there afterwards, fish-pale arms and legs gleaming in the near-dark. "We don't have to do this, if you don't want to?" He made it a question, but his voice was steady.

I took back my legs and sat up, pulling down my white cotton nightgown. The lacquered cherry headboard that had belonged to Loren's parents was cool against my shoulder blades even in the humid August night. I bunched up my pillow and wedged it behind my back.

But Loren didn't say any more. In the dark I couldn't see his face. I thought, Maybe he doesn't like it all that much either, now. And I felt cold.

I swung my legs over the side of the bed and slid down off the high mattress. I felt my way out of the room and down the dark hall and went into the bathroom to take care of myself. When I snapped on the light, my reflection in the mirror ambushed me. I had to think for a minute who it was, this woman with her lips sewn tight across, eyes smoky-edged and blank, like the holes in the quilt from Loren smoking his pipe in bed.

About then I started collecting glass paperweights—antiques, some of them, greenish or purplish like old doorknobs—with things embedded in them, flowers or insects, a dinosaur, a silver horn. The sameness of their shapes despite their different contents was comforting. Loren would look over the half-glasses he wore for close work, his hair and beard glinting red in the lamplight. "Irene," he'd say, "you have more paperweights than Pinkham has pills," coming down hard on the p's. He'd turn back to his stamps, slotting them into place, squares of blue and green and dull red, in an album with a fat leather cover that I gave him for Christmas one year, to start him collecting.

So, for the most part, we were content. Isn't that the great thing about marriage? That the bad things even out under the steady lapping of days, that the long stretch of the whole is what matters? I was a good wife. Homemaker: I made a home. When I was growing up, my mother, a good Wisconsin German, more than once made me sleep under my bed with the dustballs; I learned. And Loren appreciated it; he liked neatness and order and certainty. I belonged to the Garden Club and the Lutheran Ladies' Auxiliary, which my best friend Jenny was vice-president of. Loren went back and forth to his job at the post office and cared for the few animals we had—cows and some chickens; usually a pig as well—and did carpentry, mending and building, in his workshop out by the barn. These things marked off the days, partitioned them and gave them shape, while the seasons slid by and the years ran together like the pattern in the rose-and-blue oilcloth on my kitchen table.

The ice has begun to break up on the lake. Huge slabs are piled bluish-white along the water's edge, pushed up onto land by the water's slow action. On the bank my feet in old rubber boots sink into softening mud and dead leaves.

She grew into a tall girl, Mary Rose, sapling-skinny like the young birches across the lake, leggy as the neighbors' colts pastured at the bottom of our land. She'd come over from down the road two or three times a week. She must have been lonely—no brothers or sisters, and her mother dying when she was born. Will Klossner had all he could do to keep the farm from going under, those years; though they said he spent a lot of time in town at the Ottertail Bar and Grill, and not only in the evenings, either. I knew how it was. Growing up, nobody in Whitewater had had much; my cradle was a box, an apple box. I didn't like to interfere. She wasn't mine. But the Klossner family and Loren's had been neighbors for forty years, and so sometimes I'd call Will and, just in passing, mention that Mary Rose looked like she needed new shoes or a warmer coat, didn't children grow out of things fast though? And wasn't it hard to notice when you lived with them day in, day out?

Loren was twenty-seven when Mary Rose first saw him, and I was thirty. A man could want a child as deeply as a woman did; some men could. That was what I told myself. At first he used to make her things: tiny wooden puzzles, a dollhouse, a perpetual-motion machine out of cherry wood with silver balls that ran up and down, up and down. Then, when she was eight or so, he began to teach her. "You wouldn't believe how that child can use her hands, Irene," he said to me at the end of that first afternoon, stamping sawdust and wood-curls off his boots onto my clean kitchen floor. "She's a natural, is what she is." His face, ruddier than usual, gleamed with pleasure. Good, I thought then; it's good he has something to do that he likes, and someone to do it with. It made him look young again and light, and as if he believed in things.

I got so I counted on seeing her. I'd look out on fine days and see them together in the yard with their hacksaws and T-squares, fitting and joining and mitering. Laughter, like half-heard music. Loren's head of flaring hair close to her fair one, the two heads drawing even, as she grew taller. Once they made an oak and cherry birdfeeder with tiers like a wedding cake and carving as fancy as frosting. They were out there in front of the shed for hours a day, their two heads bent over the thing in perfect concentration.

Rapt—that was a word for her in those years. Gazing at the birds that came to the feeder; watching a new calf. Once I came on her with one of our neighbor's colts in the back pasture. It had come right up to the fence where she stood under a tall Scotch pine. Their eyes were locked. The yearling trembled lightly all over as if caught in an invisible net.

She must have felt me behind her, because she turned. The tarry smell of pine was all around us and pine needles crunched under my feet.

"Hi, Mrs. Johanssen," she said. She was always polite—well taught, for a motherless child. "Isn't he beautiful?" She hooked one arm around the colt's neck. He stood still, even when she laid her cheek against his shoulder. "Look at his coat, like silk. And his beautiful eyes." Her large hands opened and closed. "Isn't he *beautiful?*"

She sounded like any horse-crazy young girl; but her eyes held that question I could never make out.

"Yes," I said. "He is."

But they were both beautiful, standing there so close together, her pale cheek against his shiny dark skin. A sudden breeze loosened a sharp little shower of pine needles, and the colt's head came up, white rimming his eyes. She turned to soothe him. Her shoulder blades strained her plaid flannel shirt, which was too small for her; her flat butterscotch hair, never really clean, fell in clumps against her neck. Looking at her made me feel dizzy and light, as if with the next puff of wind I could blow away. I wanted to put my arms around her to anchor myself, as she had put hers around the colt, to feel her shoulder blades sharp against my breasts. It was somehow hard to pull away, to turn and go back up the hill to the house.

That night, for the first time in years, I dreamed the dream I used to have, oh, two or three times a year. I am a nurse, a midwife. White light pooling around us, and the acrid smell of blood. I'm quivering all over but steady. I can't see the mother's face beyond the mound of her belly. The whole stream of my attention has narrowed down to that one opening. Then it's there—the blue-veined head, wet hair plastered to it, round and hard as a baseball. My hands in thin plastic gloves guide it out, my two fingers make a track for the shoulders to ride out on, first one, then the other. The slippery backside thuds into my hands. Before I can even grasp the ankles to turn it over, I hear its narrow cry.

I woke up with sunlight striping the room like an Adirondack blanket and Loren humped up beside me, his back turned and his head almost covered by the worn blue summer quilt. At its edge, his dark-red hair curled. Closing my eyes again, I imagined the baby grown into a tall child standing in the ditches, in high grass threaded with wild onion and Queen Anne's lace. Rows of chigger welts embroidering the tanned skin of those long legs; head thrown back to the sun. Would it have Loren's smile, his ruddy brows that flared like wings? Beside me his quilt-covered shoulders moved slowly with his breathing.

A little wind sifts the fur trim on my parka against my cheek, light as baby fingers. As I walk the lake's edge, I remember how Jenny came to see me. I was busy with the canning—in August it's always a race between me and the tomatoes—but she stood on the mat and rang and rang until finally I had to let her in. She is small and fierce and birdlike. She darts. That day she made me feel even more like a scarecrow than usual, stiff and stolid.

She tried to talk to me. Missed you at the last couple of meetings, ought to get out more like you used to, and so on, and so on. Lighting on the edge of Loren's chair, she said earnestly, "A woman with no children." She has three, nearly grown. "Irene, you're not listening."

"I am," I said. "I'm listening." The house was filled with the wet-washrag smell of boiling fruit. Had I turned the gas off under the tomatoes?

"—with no children. You should keep up your friends. Me, for instance." I thought I could hear a rough bubbling sound coming from the kitchen. "—or you could get a job, maybe. You need other *interests*. Where your treasure lies, there will your heart be also."

Jen likes to quote the Bible; she probably knows more of it by heart than any other Lutheran in Fillmore County.

"What?" I said.

She looked up at me. Greying bangs, escaping from the pink headband she wore, fell into her eyes; humidity from all the boiling turned them into corkscrews. Her voice slowed, as if she were explaining something to a child. "Your whole life is Loren and this house. If anything happened to him, you'd be all alone."

Alone. The word struck and echoed like a dinner gong. Breathy little words like *left* and *lost* flew out around it. I listened to Jen a while longer without hearing what she said, and then I gave her coffee and shooed her out the door. I had work to do.

I think now it must have been around that time that Loren began to get more and more *absent*. When he talked to me, I felt as if he didn't see me. Who was the person he looked at and moved his mouth to send words at?

He went to bed earlier, leaving me to eat supper alone. It got to be like those Identikit things that the police give to eyewitnesses so they can select this nose, that pair of eyes, this upper lip, flipping back and forth until they put together a face that matches the one in their mind. That's what I did with Loren. Only with the whole person, not just the face.

I'd select this movement, that smile, this touch. I'd sit the whole thing up at the dining room table and put words in its mouth so it would talk to me. So Loren would tell me about his day—who got a package from New York City, how far he'd gotten with the curly maple chest. And I'd tell him about mine—church gossip I'd heard from Jenny, what seedlings were up in the garden. Over the vase of white and yellow daisies, his eyes, dark as the rubies in my wedding ring, trapped the light and held it, like water under ice.

Finally I asked him. He was at the sink washing up for supper. "Is there someone else?" I said. I sat at the kitchen table in one of Loren's mother's ladder-back chairs, afraid to breathe, afraid to lift my elbows from the oilcloth. There was a sort of blank place in my mind, empty, with the wind washing through it. What I'd meant to say was, Do you love me? It would have been the first time I'd ever brought myself to ask. But what if he just said, No. Standing there in the kettle-grey light from the window over the sink.

He went still. "Of course not. You know that." The anise odor of Lava soap pierced through the smell of corned beef and cabbage simmering on the stove.

"I'm— I don't—know that." I tried to reach across the space between us with my words. It felt as if they bounced off his broad blue-shirted back and came back at me. "Loren, I don't know that. You're different lately, you're—not there."

He turned and looked at me. He was all white lather up to the elbows. "Irene. Don't be crazy. Who could there be?"

I couldn't say it—couldn't *think* it. Behind him, framed in my red cotton curtains, the cows stood knee-deep in wet grass at the bottom of the yard. No one had brought them in.

"I don't know," I said, suddenly tired, my arms and legs heavy as wet firewood. "I don't know what got into me. I'm sorry."

He turned back to the sink. Methodically, he began to slough the lather from his arms.

Last night I saw them dancing. Loren likes to play the radio while he works on his projects. It was early evening, but Mary Rose hadn't gone home for supper. They were finishing something—a bench, I think it was. "Don't dish up till late tonight," Loren had asked me earlier in the afternoon.

The sound of the radio drew me—maybe it was louder than usual. There was something about the music, too. It wasn't the smooth, honey-sounding music that Loren likes, the kind you hear in elevators, but some bouncy, brassy stuff. I checked the roast, which crackled pinkly, still far from done. I pulled off my apron and smoothed my hair back into its knot and went outside.

It was warm for early April, but the darkening air held a chill underneath and there were small, shrunken piles of snow in the corners of the yard. The lighted shed window flung a rectangle of light onto the hard-packed dirt beneath. In it two shadows twisted, rhythmic, elongated, stretching and disappearing and filling it again. Why did I feel like an intruder in my own yard? When I got close, I stood to the side of the open window, up against the splintery boards of the shed, and looked in.

It was as if I'd been pushing hard against a door that opened suddenly from the other side. I had to grab the rough wooden sill to keep from falling. They dipped and swayed and twirled without touching. Mary Rose was lanky and awkward in her jeans. Her breasts, small and pointed under her T-shirt, were hardly more than a boy's. In the back corner of the shed, Loren's father's old radio was turned up full volume. It was a standing radio, tall as a child, with a large hole in its belly for the speaker. The music sounded ridiculous coming out of its squat, old-fashioned bulk: fast, thudding and wailing. *Jump, jump! For my love. Jump in!* Shavings and wood-curls flew up around them. When they whirled to face each other, their eyes met. Mary Rose pushed her damp flat hair back from her forehead and laughed out loud.

She made me think of the imprisonment of life in the world. She made me feel it. She made me see everything that moved—the birds at the feeder, the colt, her and Loren and me—as if it were sealed in time and place like a butterfly in a paperweight. And still she could dance. The smell of sawdust filled my nostrils like fur.

When I got back inside, I sat down at the kitchen table with my head on my arms. I felt like someone had taken off my skin and every nerve was hanging out. Through the glass of the storm door, I watched the slanting oblong of light on the ground as it emptied and filled, emptied and filled. The gritty oilcloth under my arms smelled like old rubber boots. Feelings I'd never had before, feelings I couldn't even name, swarmed over me. *Jump. Jump in.*

I stop beside a large white birch that the piled-up ice has knocked over, lying on its side half in and half out of the water, its roots obscenely exposed. Small frozen clods cling to them. I touch a smooth spot on the trunk. It is cold as silver against my palm, where the splinters from the shed windowsill last night still sting. In the tree's upper branches a few of last year's leaves, still clinging, flicker in the little wind coming off the lake. The wind carries the damp-earth smell of things opening. At my feet, the ice hisses, shrinking, settling deeper into the water.

How will it happen? She'll come the day she turns sixteen. I'll know, because Loren will have spent the whole week making a jewelry box to give her for her birthday, tailoring and smoothing and polishing until it's like a jewel itself.

She won't come to the kitchen door the way she always has. She'll come to the front. I'll open the door and she'll stand on the threshold wrapped in a man's sheepskin coat, stained and dull at the edges. Her hair, freshly washed, flying around her head in wisps; her breath coming in little frosty puffs. Frost behind her prickling on the grass, throwing off darts of light straight into my heart.

Behind me Loren will be sitting in his leather rocker by the window with the newspaper in his lap, as he's begun to do so often, gazing out at the shed. He'll have shaved off his beard. I'll have forgotten about the cleft in his chin—I haven't seen his face naked since the first year of our marriage. How beautiful he was then, rosy as a silk-shaded lamp; now only the bones will be the same, the shelf of his brow and the square jaw sweeping forward. For an instant, his eyes will meet mine, and I'll see her question in them.

Mary Rose will stand still in the doorway. Her eyes, those strange colorless eyes, will hold mine; I'll have to look up to see into them. They'll shine on me like moonlight. She won't say a word; but I'll know what she wants as clear as if she'd spoken. It will be as if a sound I can't decipher, indistinct and sweet, were threading through the room, weaving itself around the three of us. I'll feel it in my body like a shiver all over my skin.

"Mary Rose," I'll say, as if this were an ordinary day, an ordinary visit, but moving lightly, throwing the door wide.

She'll shake her head faintly and she'll smile.

I'll start toward the closet then, to get my coat. Moving light as air.

But she'll hold out her hand to *him*, those long fingers. He'll pull himself out of his chair, the seat squeaking as he leaves it, and go and stand beside her in the doorway. They'll stand there together, the two of them. The distance between us will stretch larger and larger. I'll try to say something that would throw out a line to them, but there won't be any words. The empty rocker will titter ghostlike back and forth, back and forth on the wooden floor, slower and slower until it stops.

It
Was
Humdrum

───────────────

          She picks up the phone on the second ring. She is in the kitchen anyway. "Hello?"

"Hi, babe." Juan's voice, frayed from too many cigarettes too late at night.

"I'm sorry. You have the wrong number." Maude hangs up. It's their signal for when she can't talk; but he will hate it anyway. She had to do it: Roger and Mary Lynn are both in the living room, within earshot.

Maude goes back to the sink, where she was scrubbing potatoes. She holds them in the slant of light from the window, not bothering to cut out the eyes. On the window frame above the sink she has tacked a postcard, a reproduction of a painting. A brightly colored ship, flat as paper, on a dark-green sea; in one corner a red arrow points straight out of the painting. It is called "The Ship Ready for Departure."

Roger comes into the kitchen to get some cat food for the turtles. He walks slowly with his fists clenched at his sides, the way Lynnie used to do to keep her balance when she was first learning to walk. He does not touch Maude—pat her or rub her shoulder as he usually does—communicating by this omission that he is annoyed with her. He crouches down and reaches around her without saying anything, pulls the sack out from under the sink, and goes.

She hates it when they fight without her even knowing it. She tries to work out what the fight is about. She said something wrong at breakfast. What was it? Her hands move automatically over the roast, rubbing salt and pepper into it. It was the detective, that was it: the detective Roger hired to find his mother. Maude has always thought of her as the "Long Lost Mother," L.L.M. for short. She left when Roger was two. He hasn't seen or heard from her since, except once when he was ten or so, a card with no return address, only the Florida postmark. That was it: Maude should not have said, "When they find the L.L.M., we'll have her up for a visit." Roger wanted "L.L.M." explained.

It must be terrible to lose your mother like that—or rather, to have her lose you, like an umbrella or a single glove. Even Maude's mother hung around. Maude tumbles everything, meat and potatoes, into the oven. She goes to the doorway.

Roger's back is toward her. He throws pellets of cat food into the big tank and the turtles waver to the surface and snap at them. Before Maude and Mary Lynn moved in, they were nameless; now, courtesy of Lynnie, they are No Name and Buttercup. No Name is the size of Roger's hand; Buttercup is twice as big. They started out as ordinary dime-store turtles, no bigger than a silver dollar. Knowing and sinister, they have corrugated shells and skin wrinkled like hands that have been in water too long.

Roger finishes, closes the bag deliberately, folding the top over and over. Roger is a systems analyst. He is a good man, a good father: her deliberate, methodical husband. That's why she chose him, after the years of crazy lovers, after Mary Lynn's crazy father. So why, now, is she betraying him (that would be his word) with crazy Juan? Maude thinks of the story about the duck and the scorpion. Needing to cross the river, the scorpion asks the duck to carry her on his back. No, says the duck; you will sting me and kill me. Why would I do such a stupid thing, says the scorpion reasonably. Then *I* would drown. Persuaded, the duck agrees to ferry her across. Halfway out into the river, the scorpion stings him. As they both go down, he asks her, Why did you do it? She says: Because it is my nature.

Who is she hurting, after all? Roger doesn't know; Juan doesn't care. The image of quicksilver Juan imposes itself across Roger's back. The two of them together add up to a whole person.

On the drive into Philly the next afternoon the air is heavy and sultry. All day it's been about to rain. Maude likes South Street, the crowds, black faces, noise. Getting out of the car on Spring Garden Street, remembering to lock it (it must not get stolen: that would be very hard to explain), she breathes acrid city air, life, danger.

Juan's apartment is on the second floor, three rooms opening one into the other railroad-fashion, full of stained-glass windows and wood paneling and gilt-framed mirrors that return uncertain images like questions. The wavery light gives the whole place an underwater quality. It is full of odd thrift-shop objects: as in an aquarium, you get the feeling everything is trying to look like something else.

Maude lets herself in. The kitchen is empty. She edges around the grand piano in the middle room and finds Juan in the back room, in bed, already naked. She always comes at one, when Mary Lynn goes to afternoon daycamp.

"Hi, babe." He is languorous, already most of the way through a joint. The little sudden lurches of the heart when she first sees him or hears his voice on the phone have largely abated by now. But there is still something: direct, visceral, as breathtaking as a hand on her genitals. She doesn't love him. She knows that, for an affair, it's better to choose someone you can't love; though even then it's tricky. Sex makes its own bond, one that can even sometimes (she believes this but has never experienced it) generate love.

She undresses quickly—Lynnie will be home at four—and slides into bed beside him. Juan kisses her, running his hand over her belly, hands her the last of the joint. He gets up to get another one. She watches him cross the room, his small tight buttocks round as apples. He is, simply, beautiful. In public, people turn and stare. Reflected in the huge mirror, his erection points stiffly in front of him, wavering from side to side like a divining rod. Maude thinks of marble genitals, throngs of them, museums in Rome, in Florence.

She looks down the length of her own body, stretched out straight like a medieval knight on a tombstone: belly round and a little slack since Lynnie, wide thighs, feet long and slender. She is thirty to Juan's twenty-two, a fact which only seems to matter when she isn't with him. As he gets back into bed, lines from a poem come to mind. "I like my body / When it's with your body."

She decides not to say it out loud. Juan isn't much interested in poetry, and certainly not at this moment. She fingers the small quick pulse at the base of his throat. He makes a thready noise like a wasp. Light coming in through the colored glass of the window over the bed stains their flesh deep velvety hues, like the behinds of baboons at the zoo.

Afterwards, beached, they smoke another joint, passing it back and forth between them, faintly damp. Juan gets up and plays for her, sitting naked at the grand piano. "We're a musical people," he says when he catches her looking at him, and rolls his eyes. He keeps playing—not the things he plays in restaurants, but Gershwin, Rodgers, Kern, striding, drifting in and out of jazz. His eyes are deep brown and strong, with glistening whites. His mother was Puerto Rican; his father, *quién sabe?*

The music makes her want to dance, but her body is too heavy after making love. It would be like trying to run underwater. Listening to the music, riding on it, Maude rests in the moment. With Juan she never has to come up with a plausible algorithm to explain, step by step, how she got from wherever she was to wherever she is. He never asks. *Al-go-RITHM—is not—RHYTHM*, she thinks, in time to the music. Here she has rhythm; at home, algorithm. She laughs out loud.

When she leaves, Juan walks her to the door, bare-chested in jeans, his glossy hairless skin like polished leather. What if, she thinks, driving home, what if one day she just stayed there? Stayed with Juan. She could get a job, Mary Lynn could go to school in the city; she would never have to explain anything.

The traffic makes her late. When she pulls up outside the row house, Mary Lynn is sitting on the steps, trying to entice some sparrows with crusts she must have hidden in her pockets at lunch.

"Mary Lynn, *don't* do that." But Mary Lynn's attention has already moved on.

"Look, Ma." Lately she has taken to calling Maude that. "Look, Ma. That's *nature*." A black ant, shiny and fat, crawls slowly across the stoop, drugged by the heat. "Can I go under the sprinkler? It's so hot." Mary Lynn looks straight up at Maude, her forehead corrugating with the intensity of her desire. She has Maude's wild red hair, her father's brown eyes.

"Yes. Run up and change, and I'll turn it on."

Mary Lynn glitters under the fine spray, drops flashing off her arrow-straight body as she jumps and turns. At six, she is as straight up and down as a boy. "Come in," she cries and beckons with quick gestures. Maude laughs, shakes her head. It's more pleasurable just to look at Lynnie. She remembers the pure sensual joy of having a very small child, the feel and smell of Lynnie at one and two and three, a hundred small daily pleasures. How could the L.L.M. have relinquished that?

When Mary Lynn has had enough, they go in. Mary Lynn takes off her bathing suit. Maude dries her small body and wraps it in a yellow towel. She puts on "Saturday Night Fever." They sit in the kitchen drinking Kool-Aid the same violent pink as Mary Lynn's bathing suit.

"Let's dance," says Mary Lynn when they finish. They push the table and chairs into the corner and dance wildly, twirling and flinging each other around. *Oh, oh, oh, oh: stayin' alive. Stayin' alive.* When the song ends, they collapse together on the floor, breathless. Maude rewraps the naked Mary Lynn in her towel.

"Okay, Bean-Bag. Go get dressed." She gives her a thump on her toweled behind.

"Don't *call* me that. I'm too *old*."

"Oh," Maude sighs. She buries her face in her daughter's damp hair. "What'll I do when you grow up and leave me?"

"You and Roger have your chother." When Mary Lynn was smaller, she heard the phrase "each other" as "our chother"; she still thinks of a chother as some mysterious secretion that grows between two people and cements them together. She adds craftily, "You could have another baby."

"Nothing doing."

The front door opens. Mary Lynn struggles free and runs to greet Roger. The record clicks off.

The sudden silence is gummy and bland. There is so much silence in Maude's life with Roger. Whole happenings go on inside it, subterranean complications and resolutions that Maude never even knows about until they're over. Sometimes he tells her there was something wrong between them last week, or last month, but everything's all right now. It's like finding half a worm in an apple.

Roger comes into the kitchen. He turns his lips inside-out when he kisses her. She hopes she doesn't smell of marijuana. He always kisses her hello and goodbye: it's part of his algorithm. "How was your day?" she says.

He tells her in detail while she gets out a beer for him. (She does not have to ask what he wants.) Maude feels as if she has been absorbed; she feels contained, like a ship in a bottle, like Jonah in the belly of the whale. She thinks, He has swallowed me.

"Have you heard anything about—" she catches herself in time, "your mother?"

"No." He looks grim. She is sorry she asked. In a few minutes Roger sets down the half-finished beer and gets up and goes down the hall to their bedroom, where he will lie on top of the puffy dacron bedspread and stare out the window. They have run out of conversation anyway, all the routine inquiries ticked off. She thinks of Juan—passionately, volubly (erratically, untruthfully) communicative.

———— ————

Even in dreams, Roger doesn't speak. Maude does. At first she was afraid she would say Juan's name in her sleep; but as time goes by, and she apparently doesn't, she relaxes. The thought occurs to her: perhaps she has said it, and Roger hasn't wanted to bring it up. Sometimes she thinks it's not that Roger doesn't understand her but that he understands her too well. (She imagines a traveling salesman trying to pick up a woman with the plea, "My wife understands me.")

Now, lying beside Roger while he sleeps, Maude listens to the occasional thump of the turtles moving in the tank. Her thoughts spiral out into the darkness. Often now, she feels unfaithful when she makes love with her husband. Sometimes she pretends he's Juan. She exchanges his crisp curly hair for Juan's silky stuff, his hairy chest for Juan's smoothness. But something always breaks the spell. She feels his beard; or her eyes open inadvertently. Then she just hangs on and tries to remember the algorithm for making love. Afterwards, the kisses, small pats, the murmurs of endearment and sighs of success are hard to stay still through.

She gets up and takes a shower. Then she goes into the kitchen and makes a cup of tea and sits at the narrow counter with it. She looks at her reflection in the dark windows of the old rowhouse, the glass grainy with age like taffeta. Maybe if Roger weren't *around* so much. He's always there, wants to spend all their free time together, comes home early to be with her. Closing the bathroom door makes him uneasy: she can feel his heavy presence outside it, waiting. She feels as if she were pushing him through life in a shopping cart, pointing out this delight, wheeling him up to that pleasure. His first wife left him for somebody else, just like that, no warning. He came home one day and she was gone. "She was young and restless," Roger said when he told Maude about it. He made it sound like a tautology, as if youth and restlessness were the same thing. Maude pictures her bounding, freckled, with bright hair in a single thick braid down her back. Thinking about her makes Maude feel old.

Whereas Roger makes her feel young. "Listen, Mother," she said when she called to say she was getting married at last. "He isn't young, and he isn't pretty." By that time her mother's standards had fined down to minimal: a husband (any husband) for her daughter; a father for her granddaughter, who, miraculously, was not black.

"Your father would be so glad. A steady man. A good steady job." Maude doesn't really remember her father, who died when she was five. Just an outline, like the line drawings you see painted on city sidewalks: burly, broad-shouldered, big hands. Roger is about the same size and shape.

Really, Maude thinks now, Mother thought we would live in Fort Washington or somewhere and have a pair of golden retrievers with golden, stupid eyes. She puts her cup in the sink and turns out the light. She thinks of all the men, her lovers, a long chain stretching across the years of high school, college, dropping out, odd jobs. She lost count somewhere around thirty; jobs, sooner than that. All the changing, the different selves; and at each juncture a man would appear who represented the next self, the next Maude. Lynnie's father was the last. Intense, passionate, unpredictable, sometimes he would hit Maude or choke her, then afterwards sprawl on the floor in an agony of contrition, seizing her ankles, while the baby watched with wide eyes. By the time he left, Maude had already met Roger.

Maude goes back to bed. In the night she dreams of Juan's underwater cave of an apartment, of the two of them swimming strongly in the tangled sheets.

They hear from the detective. They get a card from the L.L.M. herself. It is a diffident, impersonal card with a prefabricated greeting, "Thinking of You." Inside are the time and day and flight number, with the handwritten message, "Dear Son, Am looking forward to seeing You again after so Many Years."

Roger lies on the bed and looks out the window. He sleeps a lot, sleeping at Maude, who can't figure out what she's done. The phrase "L.L.M." hasn't crossed her lips since the detective's phone call. She has been careful how she refers to this woman who now looms in their lives, dwarfing everything else.

Mary Lynn tries to work out what to call her. Harriet, since she's not a blood relation, just as she calls Roger Roger and not Daddy? Lately Mary Lynn has been interested in blood. On the other hand, she'd like another grandmother. Grandmothers buy you Barbie dolls and tell you you swim better than the boys. Mary Lynn makes Maude help her draw a family tree. Red for blood relationships: Maude, Maude's mother; green for "Steps": Roger, Harriet. Black, wonders Maude, for absent members? Her father; Lynnie's?

A week before she's due to arrive in Philadelphia, the L.L.M. sends a photograph. It shows a young woman of nineteen or twenty in a glamor pose, full length, one leg curving inward at the knee. She is wearing a bathing suit, draped and boned in the style of the forties, and her hair marches across her head in precisely crimped formation. Her full lips are very dark. Contemplating this Betty Grable image with Mary Lynn looking over her shoulder, Maude cannot reconcile it with that of the seventy-year-old woman living on the edge of poverty in a tiny Florida town. The detective has told Roger her story:

fourth (fourth? thinks Maude) husband dead, no insurance, no pension. When she was young, the L.L.M. was a singer. She sang with bands in Cleveland and Pittsburgh and Cincinnati.

In the days before she comes, the silence between Maude and Roger grows thick and sluggish as the late summer weather. It spreads and fills the corners of the house. Maude tries, as hard as Roger himself usually does, not to fight. Fighting with him, even a small fight over nothing, would be like opening a door onto an elevator shaft. She would end up telling him about Juan, thrusting at him the fact of her lover, in anger or in guilt, she's not sure which. If they start at all, she will find herself falling, falling.

With relief she sees Roger drive off to the airport. The weather breaks at last, the heavy August sky cracks open and releases rain.

When they get back, it is the tail end of the thunderstorm. For hours the rain has been beating city dirt into the pavement and hurling itself against the old windows of the row house. It is very late. The storm delayed the plane, made the drive back on the Schuylkill Expressway a nightmare. Maude barely has time to register how small she is, this woman who has dominated their lives for weeks— how thin and small her outstretched hand. Harriet is very tired: they will talk tomorrow.

When Maude comes downstairs in the morning, Harriet is already up, fully dressed, sitting in one of the straight-backed chairs in the living room. Her hands make fists on the chair arms. Maude can't think for a minute who she reminds her of; then she remembers how Roger walks.

"Good morning," Maude says. "Did you sleep well?"

"Yes, thank you. Very well."

At a loss, they look at each other. Morning light washes the room, gold overlaid with green. What can they possibly say? Everything, words that touch the heart's core—or nothing. Choices made decades ago, before Maude existed, crowd into the gap between them. Then Harriet smiles. Her skin, pale as parchment, stretches precariously over the brittle armature of bone. She reminds Maude of a cryptic construction Lynnie brought home from art class in the spring, tissue paper over a framework of toothpicks.

Maude goes into the kitchen to start the coffee, comes back to ask, "How was the trip?" The flight was rough; the weather; the whole trip took longer than Harriet expected. She smokes as if she were knitting, transferring the cigarette from hand to hand, back and forth to her mouth, in an intricate semaphore. Otherwise she sits motionless. When she talks she makes no gestures, no waving to show how fast, no spreading of her hands to show how big. Maude thinks that she is, not relaxed, but contained: in one piece, all of a piece.

When Mary Lynn comes down, Maude goes back into the kitchen. It's Saturday, so they'll have eggs and bacon and fruit. She is so hard, Maude thinks. *Crack!* She knocks an egg on the side of the blue mixing bowl and drops it in. Imagines a baby's skull. *Crack!* I can't stay with this husband. *Crack!* Not this one either. In her mind a picture forms of Harriet in Florida. Palm trees rise abruptly through the shimmering heat. Exotic birds make their exotic noises: parrots, macaws with glittering beaks. Harriet has friends, women alone like her; they play bridge on Tuesday and Thursday afternoons. She goes to the A & P in elastic stockings, into the cold slap of air-conditioned air, coaxes the shining cart up and down the aisles.

Maude looks down into the bowl. The yolks stare facelessly up at her. She counts them—ten eggs for four people? She sees the picture of Saint Lucy, virgin martyr, on the calendar of her childhood. When Lucy refused to yield (her body, not her soul), they put out her eyes. In the picture, she holds a platter with her upturned eyes on it like two fried eggs. From the dining room Maude hears Mary Lynn's thin tuneless whistle, her voice explaining Harriet to the turtles. They are feeding them grapes, which Roger has asked her not to do. Maude puts rice in the salt-shaker as Roger has taught her, so that the humidity doesn't keep the salt from flowing, picking up the fine grains carefully between her fingernails. She admires them in passing: long nails, smooth as ivory, smooth hands that would not make anyone think of parchment.

At breakfast Harriet sits across from Mary Lynn, Maude across from Roger. Mary Lynn and Maude are still in their bathrobes. Harriet sits straight in her careful dark-red knit suit with a darned place over one elbow and her careful hair, protected last night by plastic pleated like an accordion.

"What's that painting there?" she asks. "Who did it?"

"Guy Anderson." Roger is pleased to be asked. He turns and looks

at the painting with satisfaction. When he bought it, the gallery reg-
istered him as the owner. He has papers on it, like a pedigreed animal.

"Very nice." Harriet looks around, making a gesture with her eyes
only, to include everything in the room. "You have a nice home."

Maude looks at Roger, then at Harriet. She is his mother. It's a
connection that you can't break, that you can always resume, like the
Law of Return in Israel. Maude thinks of the word for it: inalienable.
She wonders if Roger will ask the question. Maybe he's decided not
to disturb things. The first maxim of computer programming, he has
told her, is: If it works, don't fix it.

As if he's read her thoughts, Roger says into a lull, "Mother."
Harriet looks up. "Why did you leave—my father?" He doesn't
say, me.

She hesitates. Her hands make a sudden small motion. She says,
"It was humdrum."

Maude's stomach gives a throb like a bass fiddle. Roger turns to
look at her as if he feels the vibration. His eyes move from her face
to his mother's; they hold an emotion she cannot read.

After breakfast Roger and Mary Lynn and Harriet leave for the
zoo, Lynnie holding Harriet's hand. If they hurry, Lynnie tells her
grandmother, they'll be in time to see the nocturnal mammals get
their dish of blood.

Alone, Maude stands in the quiet house. Harriet is whole. Like the
scorpion, she has followed her nature. Whole-hearted; hard-hearted.
Are the two things the same? And she, Maude—is she split in two,
living her life on two parallel tracks that never meet, while Roger
watches from his shell of silence, keeping her safe, waiting for her
to leave?

When the dishes are done, she leaves them gleaming in the rack
and goes into the living room. She puts on "Saturday Night Fever"
and turns the volume up high. Walls and floors and furniture vibrate
faintly to the deepest rhythms. Slowly and deliberately she takes off
her clothes and lays them across one end of the sofa. She runs her
hands through her hair. She dances in the green-gold light.

The
White
Hope of
Cleveland

The summer before I started high school, the summer of 1962, was the hottest Philadelphia had ever seen. My mother would send me out before breakfast with a basket of wash while the dew steamed off the grass. By ten o'clock the wash would be dry. I could feel it drying as I hung it up, prying open the stiff folds locked in by the washer, snapping on the wooden clothespins. My bare feet were cold and wet, the sun burned the top of my head.

As I reached and hung, reached and hung, I thought dark thoughts about manual labor, which I surely wasn't meant for; though what I *was* meant for eluded me. That year my face and body were changing faster than I could take in. Looking in the mirror, which I did frequently to take soundings, what I saw was never what I wanted:

hair like ginger ale, pale and fizzy; glasses; eyes behind them too large and dark. I wanted to look like my friend Roberta, who had pale-red hair and pale, freckled skin fitted neatly over narrow bones and blue eyes that slanted like a fox's. As far back as fifth grade, boys had liked her.

At midsummer my grandfather came up from El Paso, his first visit without my grandmother, who'd died in March. After he retired and they moved south, he and my grandmother had spent a couple of weeks every summer in our big house on the Main Line, going on to my uncles and cousins in Cleveland and St. Louis, then looping back to Texas. Each year the visit lasted longer. For the first time in his life, my grandfather (according to my mother) had discovered his family. Too late for his children, who had embedded themselves in lives of their own; but we grandchildren adored him.

That year my grandfather drove up alone, despite my mother's arguments with him on the telephone, her insistence that he was getting too old. He drove the big navy-blue Buick he had had ever since I could remember. It was air-conditioned, which I thought was very exotic. A Saint Christopher medal hung from the rearview mirror; a small sticker in the fly window on the passenger side entitled the driver, in English and Spanish, to use the town dump.

The high spot of my grandparents' visits had always been the trip my grandfather and I made, just the two of us, to the book department of Wanamaker's. I was his favorite grandchild. He didn't like either of my sisters, and my cousins on my mother's side were all boys whose fathers were a disappointment, one a cabdriver, the other working in the steel mills. I knew without being told that my mother was jealous of my grandfather's affection for me. There were no book-buying sprees when she was growing up: instead, an often absent father who lived for his work.

That summer, instead of driving, we took the train into Center City. It was a relief to get out of the house, out of the silence and the chill which at the time I associated with my grandmother's death; away from Rhoda and aggravating Althea. I sat across from my grandfather in the seats at the front of the car, the only ones facing each other, and we read our books. That summer I was reading William James's *Principles of Psychology*. It was too old for me; but my mother never noticed things like that, and my father seemed to be away on business a lot of the time now. My grandfather read Mickey

Spillane, holding the book out in front of him; it looked small in his big, large-knuckled hands. I could see his Adam's apple bobbing up and down.

Our family albums held yellowed newspaper clippings with photographs of my grandfather in the ring before a fight, towering over his coach. His skinny chest looked stark above the dark boxing shorts, and his hands, larger in boxing gloves, bloomed unexpectedly out of long thin limbs. The headlines called him the White Hope of Cleveland. He must have been pretty good, because he put himself through college and law school by boxing, and he was already married with children then. Before that, an orphan or a runaway (we were never sure), he did odd jobs and slept in doorways until the nuns at Saint Joseph's took him in.

He looked to me now as if he had shrunk, as if the loss of my grandmother had diminished him. He wore the clothes of the larger man he had been: wrinkled blue-striped seersucker jacket, shoulders too broad; linen pants with the cuffs puddling over his shoes. The pants were the color of vanilla ice cream.

After a while he looked up. "What are you reading, Lil?" I held up my book to show him. He nodded. "Good man, James. Knew how to put things."

"Well. Some of it I don't absolutely understand." I wouldn't have admitted this to anyone else.

"Neither do a lot of people. What so wild as words are?"

"What?"

"Browning, Lil.

> 'What so wild as words are,
> I and thou
> In debate as birds are,
> Hawk on bough.'"

I didn't know what to make of this but didn't want to let such a grown-up conversation lapse. I was sure he'd never talked like this with my mother. "It sounds like you in the courtroom," I said. "In debate as birds are."

"With the judge as the hawk?" He smiled. "Well, not quite. But, you know, Lil, a lawyer's real stock in trade is words. Words are what convince a jury. A good argument can set an innocent man free. Why, a *good* argument can set a *guilty* man free."

I was startled. This possibility had never occurred to me. "Did you ever defend somebody who was guilty?"

He nodded. "Many times. Many times."

"Did you know he was guilty?"

"Yes, Lil. Often I did. They'd tell me, you see. If I was going to defend them I had to know everything."

I looked out the window so he wouldn't see that I was shocked. Telephone poles shot past, one after another, with little whickering sounds. "What about—justice?" I said, keeping my voice cool and even.

"Justice is this, Lil. You try as hard as you can to defend your man; the other lawyer tries as hard as he can to convict him. That's how blind Blind Justice is. You each load up her scales with your words, and the one who weighs in the heaviest wins. Justice isn't something ordained by the Almighty beforehand. It's whatever you make the jury see. Eloquence, that's what justice is. Eloquence."

This sounded dangerously wrong, but interesting. I put it away to look at later. "Haverford's next," I said, "then Narberth." My grandfather looked at me for a moment, then smiled and picked up his book. I went back to reading about the relationship between the mind and the physical brain, silently rolling the word "epiphenomenon" around in my mouth like a marble. I pictured the mind rising off a mass of neurons like steam off the grass.

One stop before Reading Terminal a group of high-school kids got on. The girls moved confidently down the aisle, translating the rocking of the car into a sexy swagger that didn't hang implausibly on their bodies the way it would have on mine. Their voices filled the car. "Where *you* goin', man?" "What you got?" Two of the boys beat intricate patterns on the worn leather seats, slapping their palms down fast and hard, cutting through the rhythm of the wheels on the track. Across the aisle from us a girl who looked a little like Roberta sat down tight against her boyfriend and lifted his arm to drape it around her shoulders. Shooting them a look of annoyance, my grandfather read on; but I couldn't. I felt drawn toward them, almost but not quite wishing I were with them instead of with him.

At Reading Terminal we got off and made our way through the confusion out onto Market Street, city smells steaming up from the pavement. My T-shirt stuck to my back and my glasses kept sliding down my nose. We inserted ourselves into the crowd. As we walked I recited to myself: Market-Chestnut-Walnut-Locust-Spruce-Pine— the streets east of City Hall in order, a rhythm Rhoda and I used to jump rope to.

The mahogany coolness of Wanamaker's was a relief. Elevators, like neckties, made my grandfather uncomfortable; so we swept along on escalators of an intimidating steepness until we reached the eighth floor. Between narrow aisles, expanses of books on tables stretched out in front of us. Huge black-and-white photographs of famous writers hung on chains from the ceiling. I felt dizzy with possibilities.

"Choose whatever you want," said my grandfather, edging away toward Crime. "As many as you like."

Before we left, my mother had taken me aside as usual and made me promise to limit myself to five. I had never told my grandfather about this limit; he must have thought I had remarkable self-control, though seven years of report cards from Most Precious Blood said otherwise. Half of each report was devoted to academic subjects and half to "Traits." OBEDIENCE: *Cheerfully obeys rules and regulations both of church and school; is at the right place at the right time ready for work; has work completed on time. SELF-CONTROL: Usually thinks before acting; restrains hasty impulses.* I did all right on Obedience, Perseverance, Courage, and Health Habits. But in Self-Control I always got B's, a bad grade for a girl. "Too independent," Sister Inez Cecilia had written in the margin this past June, even though (or because) Reverend Mother was having me skip eighth grade and graduate a year early. In high school we wouldn't have Traits.

My mother knew my grandfather wouldn't set any limits, not like he'd set them with her. He was the one who'd decided that for my mother it would be secretarial school, not college and law school and following in her adored father's footsteps. It was the Depression; the money was needed for the boys. My mother went to work in the front office at Ellisco, where she moved with a slight stoop, shoulders hunched to hide the breasts she thought were too big, until my father came in one day to complain about a desk that had been delivered without any drawers. She didn't understand the family she married into—melancholy, unimaginative, and Protestant—and she couldn't make them understand her. She held her own in her own way, indulging in small, cryptic acts of rebellion. She sent her daughters to Catholic schools, to the dismay of the people I used to think of, when I was small, as the Other Grandparents. She hung her wash out on the line.

Within fifteen minutes I'd found as many books. I went for expensive hardcover ones that cost two-fifty or three dollars and were too old for me. That day I discovered *The Birds Fall Down*, and for weeks afterward I was a seventeen-year-old Russian *émigrée* with beautiful hair.

My grandfather paid for my choices. The clerk gave me a shopping bag with handles because we'd bought so many, and we began the long careening descent to the main floor.

The revolving door popped us out into the humid air. After we'd gone a block down Chestnut Street, my grandfather said, "You know, Lil, you look more like your grandmother every time I see you."

"What was she like when she was young?"

"Oh. She was—not beautiful. No, she wasn't a beautiful woman. But she had eyes like the skies over Ireland. Eloquent eyes." My grandfather had never been to Ireland: maybe the nuns had told him about the wide, grey skies mottled with clouds. Certainly he wasn't thinking of the sooty skies over Sosnowiec, the small mining town where my grandmother had grown up. In the family album those wide, calm eyes looked out from my grandmother's wedding photograph, huge in the bony face. At sixteen she'd run away to America to escape an arranged marriage; she came to her married sister in Cleveland and worked in a bakery. I'd often imagined their first meeting across the long fragrant loaves, he with his blue suit, blue eyes, blue-black Irish hair.

As we stepped into the street against the light, my grandfather sighed, a long shallow breath. "More like Ilona every year. Your grandmother," he added, as if I might have forgotten who we were talking about, or as if I knew a lot of Ilonas. He walked carefully, keeping a close watch on the pavement. I took his arm and steered him out of the path of an oncoming car and up onto the curb.

My grandfather slept for most of the train ride back, his head tucked to one side. His white hair was still thick and crisp. In spite of the coconut-oil hairdressing it curled wildly in the humidity, Catholic hair, not like my father's disciplined hair that held neat furrows from his comb. Mickey Spillane slid out of his hands and fell to the floor. I picked it up and brushed the grit from its pages and laid it on the seat.

I had to wake him when the conductor called our stop. We always finished our excursions with ice cream at the restaurant near the station; but this time he almost walked past it.

"Wait," I said. "Don't you want ice cream?"

"Of course. Of course." He tried to look as if he'd been just about to turn.

The restaurant was owned by my friend Roberta's father. Inside the door were a jukebox and a machine that checked your heart rate. We sat down at the counter opposite a long mirror etched with famous men's profiles and draped in an American flag. Roberta, wearing an air of pleased self-consciousness, was waiting on customers. "May I help you?" she asked, then added out of the corner of her mouth, in parentheses, "Hi, Lil."

I introduced her to my grandfather, and we ordered: vanilla for him; butter pecan for me. While we waited for our ice cream, a mouse ran out from under the counter and paused, looking up with bright eyes. I nudged my grandfather, but in the second it took him to look, the mouse disappeared.

We ate in silence. The anticipatory pleasure of the books mingled with the present pleasure of the ice cream smooth and bright in my mouth. I watched Roberta move deftly back and forth. Her hair was sleeked back into a little ball imprisoned in a beaded hairnet.

Between customers she came and leaned proprietarily on the counter across from us. "So, how's your week been, Lil?"

"Okay." Her narrow light eyes wore a fringe of mascara. I said, "You look good."

"I keep telling you." Her eyes moved across my face, mouth nose eyes, up to my hair. "If you got contacts. You could be cute. Boys like blondes."

Of course I hated my glasses. But, dutifully, I wore them (OBEDIENCE), kept them on when they steamed up in winter and slid down my nose in summer (PERSEVERANCE).

My grandfather, who had been listening to our conversation in silence, snorted. I pushed my elbow against his arm; but he spoke anyway. "*Cute.*" Little drops of spit flew out of his mouth with the word. He reached over and pushed my glasses back up on my nose. I wanted to slide off the stool and under the counter with the mouse.

A customer beckoned then, and Roberta went off. My grandfather and I finished our ice cream. We went out into the still, glittering heat of late afternoon.

At home I went past the living room, where my parents sat in newspapered silence, into the bathroom and locked the door. Standing in the shaft of light from the high window by the sink, I took off my glasses and looked in the mirror. As usual my reflection gave me a little quick shock, like when someone shakes you out of sleep. I pulled my hair back with both hands and narrowed my eyes like a fox's; but it was no use.

Eyes like the skies over Ireland. My grandfather had offered me a choice, the choice he hadn't been able to give my mother. That was his gift to me, a generation late.

"Lil, that you?" Althea jerked the doorknob back and forth. "Let me in."

It wasn't what I wanted. I did not want to choose. If eloquence was justice, might it not also be beauty? Reflected behind me, in the shadowed corners of the room, I imagined my photograph hanging from Wanamaker's eighth-floor ceiling on a chain. In it I would be beautiful; and behind it would lie my words, which would make people see. My life, in which justice and beauty would rise off the surface of the everyday, like steam off the grass on a summer morning.

"Lil! I gotta *pee.*"

I straightened my shoulders and let go of my hair. In the mirror my own eyes looked back at me.

Imagined Colors

On the last night in May I lay beside my wife listening to the sound of her quiet snoring. Faith, who when we first slept together was so still that I sometimes laid my hand on her to make sure she was breathing, the way she would do with Donny and Joe when they were born. In every room my clocks were ticking, not quite in time, syncopated. I restore old clocks for a hobby. Evenings and weekends, at my long lighted table in the basement, I sand down finials, polish spandrels, clean and fit the delicate shining gears. The only room in the house without clocks is the bathroom.

Falling asleep seemed to take longer each night, and when I did manage it, my sleep would be fractured by dreams. Night after night, the same dreams, fault lines along which my sleep repeatedly cracked and broke. Now I tried squinting into the sound-filled darkness, willing a picture the way Faith learned to do when she was a child, to make herself fall asleep. (My Faith has always lived in images. The pictures in her head make a world that's as real to her as the one she lives in—realer.) Out of the darkness I tried to construct a jungle-scape: the round eyes of the great cats; the sly, human faces of the baboons. I tried to people it with the ardent women who go for ten or fourteen or twenty years out into the bush. Jane Goodall, Mary Leakey—I placed them with the animals, luminous and unmoving in the green stillness. But the women—restless explorers, pioneers with sharp faces and sharp eyes—refused to stay put.

What does a man do when he wants to understand something? I am a statistician, and what I do is watch. I know how to observe, not how to make things happen. Of course, for statistics to work, you have to have all the facts. As Marty, my boss at Boston Preferred Insurers, says, you have to get your ducks lined up. After that, though, it's a matter of waiting.

I put my hand on Faith's shoulder and pushed her gently over onto her left side. The snoring stopped. The animals and their green jungle disappeared.

Here's what I knew:

1. Faith had begun to talk a lot about the life-drawing class she'd started at the DeCordova the month before
2. The class met once a week, on Tuesday nights
3. Once a week, on Tuesday nights, my wife's face was flushed and her hair sprang out in a froth of tender curls across her forehead, contradicting the lines in it, and she hummed under her breath in the kitchen.

Those were the facts I had. I did nothing. I calculated, extrapolated, made my projections; and then I waited.

"Housework is like alcohol," my reconstituted mother said to Faith. "Every time you do it, some brain cells are destroyed."

When she wagged her head for emphasis, the large hoops in her ears, the exact red of her cotton jumpsuit, banged against her jaw. She speared a slice of tomato and made a single mouthful of it.

"I do a lot of other things, Mother A. There's my job at the library—"

"Sorting and stacking," said my mother, who doesn't think much of catalogue librarians, or any other kind of librarians, for that matter. For years she sat in the kitchen weeping and reading theology, while her children, seven of us, raised each other; when my youngest brother started school, she went to work as a window designer for Filene's in Brookline. One day a week she comes to each child's house for dinner, which she no longer cooks herself.

"—you know that," Faith went on as if my mother hadn't spoken. "And there's life class."

"Life class? So what do they teach you about life?"

"Life *drawing*, Mother," I said, and Faith said at the same time, "Drawing from life. We draw live models, that's all."

At that moment Donny knocked over his Batman mug. Faith jumped up from her chair and ran into the kitchen for a fistful of paper towels. When she started to mop up the milk pooling on the wooden table, my mother reached over and took the paper towels out of her hands.

"Here," she said to Donny. "You do it."

Donny swabbed with a seven-year-old's concentration. Joey looked around the table in pleased surprise. "It wasn't me," he said.

Faith got up and began collecting plates, piling silverware on clean-picked chicken bones. "Donald, would you put the boys to bed," she said over her shoulder, starting for the kitchen with a stack of dishes. "Your mother and I will clean up. We can have dessert after."

"Oh, do it later," my mother said. "Let's see your drawings." She flicked her cigarette and grey ash peppered her untouched slice of peach pie.

Faith demurred, but my mother insisted. Finally, rolling her eyes at me (the first time she'd looked straight at me since we'd sat down to eat), Faith put the dishes down and went to get the drawings.

"I wish she wouldn't smoke in here," she muttered as she passed my chair.

She came back with the big cardboard portfolio under her arm. Taking out the pad of newsprint, she began flipping the thin sheets.

A faint rosy flush climbed along her cheeks and across her forehead, and when she looked up, her brown eyes were oddly light.

"These were only two-minute poses," she said. "But these—" She stopped at one in which the model seemed to be lying on her stomach, elbows propped on a squarish shape (a cushion?), legs improbably twined in the air behind her.

"Well," my mother said.

The small silence hardened and swelled, like a boil.

"Very nice," I said finally. Faith never knows when I'm lying. Still, I was careful to keep my voice smooth.

Joey said, "Is it a nemperor?"

"A what?" Faith looked down at his face. "Oh. An emperor? No. Why, honey?"

"It doesn't got clothes on."

"Have," I said.

"Ugh," said Donny. "It's *naked*?"

"Pajamas, guys," I said. "Let's go. Say goodnight to Nana."

It was eight o'clock. My clocks began to fill the house with bright mechanical sound, spinning out string after string of chimes. No cuckoo clocks. I may be a romantic, but I am not whimsical.

Think of it: the studio. The sights and sounds and smells, like a warm bath for all the senses. I saw it as clearly as if I'd been there.

The dark-green Toyota pulls into the museum grounds too early. Faith parks looking out over a low grassy rise and listens to jazz on the old car's uncertain radio. A cloud of small insects spirals up in the long light from the setting sun. Their glittering movement seems to follow the rhythm of the piano. As she watches, a white moth rises slowly through their midst.

In the studio the same music is playing. Other students shuffle noisily into the bare, echoing room, choose places around the platform, clattering their easels. They are not all younger than Faith. The instructor calls the roll. He is tall and very thin and wears the kind of sandals that look as if you've put them on backwards. Faith dislikes his flat Maine voice. Carefully she deploys her charcoal—vine and pressed, soft and hard—on the ledge of her easel, along with a blend-

ing stump and a kneaded rubber eraser. She remembers molding these erasers into small phallic shapes under her desk at school.

The model's buttocks gleam, her heavy breasts shift and spread against floor, arm, pillow: a series of two-minute poses, to warm up. Faith draws. After twenty years the old movements come back slowly. The sound of water running in the studio sink mingles with the music.

"Good. That line from the throat along the shoulder." The instructor's voice pulls her to the surface. "Watch where the thigh comes forward and down. Those shadows. They're darker."

She nods without turning. He moves on to the man at the next easel, a black man, older, in a kind of apron made from a white towel threaded onto a hoop around his waist. "That leg is longer. Look. See how the foot comes toward you."

The instructor's name is Basker. Michael Basker is his name.

At the break, the model puts on her blue-and-white Japanese robe as if to declare herself a person, not a body, and goes from easel to easel inspecting. Michael Basker makes them turn their easels around so everyone can see everyone else's work. The younger students go out onto the porch to smoke. The smell of marijuana mixes with the vibrant scent of oil paint.

In the middle of the last pose of the night, a long forty-minute pose, Faith feels Michael Basker standing behind her. "Find the spine—Faith, is it? That's it, go from there."

His presence is like a force field (if Faith understands what they are; she's never been entirely sure). He is handsome. He is not handsome. She feels pulled off balance as he moves away.

I let myself in the front door without a sound. I'd stopped at Peterson's Second Hand on my way home from work. Under my arm, in a brown paper bag, was a rosewood beehive clock, 1840s I was sure, the castle wheel and pinions scabbed with rust but probably sound. I could already feel the chalk-brush between my fingers, the dark-red wood turning warm in my hands.

It was Tuesday. In the living room Faith sat reading to Donny and Joe in the big green wing chair. The top of her head, with her frizzy light-brown hair gathered up into a barrette, just cleared the back of the chair. I couldn't see the boys. She was finishing *The Night Visitors*, Donny's favorite.

"Mommy? What are you afraid of?" Donny asked. The curly knob of hair bobbed, startled; but his voice held a purely theoretical interest.

"Cellar stairs without backs. The unknown hand reaching up to grab the unwary ankle." Faith must have demonstrated by grabbing each boy: they shrieked happily.

"*I'm* afraid of three things," said Joe importantly. His small fat hand appeared at the side of the chair. "Sliding board. High diving board. Roller coaster." Ticking them off on his fingers, he held up four.

"That's heart-rendering," said Donny.

I opened and closed the front door again, loud this time. The boys scrambled down from the wing chair and ran out into the hall. They surrounded me, hurled themselves against me, climbed me like a tree. Faith came and stood in the archway between the hall and the living room, in jeans and an old white T-shirt without a logo. She leaned against a fake stucco pillar, not looking at me.

"I came home early," she said to my left ear. She looked guilty, if guilt is measured in rosiness, shininess, curl.

Brushing past me, she went upstairs to our bedroom, where she spent a lot of time lately with the door closed. Passing, I'd hear the middle drawer of the old mission-oak dresser open and shut. The frame is warped, and the gliders groan. She's a woman who saves up her dreams one by one like grains of rice in a jar, my Faith. In the middle drawer on her side of the dresser, in a nest of underwear and winter pajamas, are all her keepsakes.

I breathed in Joey's reassuring smell, dry and sweet as grass. I hadn't been prepared for it to hurt. Pain had had no place on my list of facts.

That was the fifth Tuesday.

This is how I pictured it every Tuesday night, the same ingredients:

1. the heavy fragrant air
2. July heat multiplied by a dozen fiercely concentrating bodies
3. the plunging yellow lights (before class, Michael Basker focuses and refocuses them, cursing the custodians)
4. the tumbling apples, pears, grapes of the model's flesh, abundant and gleaming
5. music.

Once it is the "Blue Danube." "Don't it just make you want to get up and skate?" says the black man next to Faith. The class has progressed from charcoal to pastels. He wipes his hands on his apron, streaking olive green and vermilion across the white toweling.

At her shoulder Michael Basker reminds Faith to shade primary areas first—the clefts where thighs or breasts or buttocks meet, the triangular cave of crossed legs when the model sits tailor-fashion on the bare wood floor. "Try some color there." He hands her the violet chalk, then, incomprehensibly, yellow ochre.

Faith says, "But—they aren't there. Those colors. I don't see them."

He is close enough for her to smell the fragrance of his fine dark-brown hair, something edible—avocados, or coconut. "You have to imagine them into that shadow," he tells her severely. "Imagine them, and you'll see them."

She imagines how his hair would feel sifting through her fingers, dense and fine as ashes.

On the break he comes outside to find her. She is standing a little apart from the others in the humid night air. They talk, about matters of technique, about an exhibit on Newbury Street that Michael thinks she should see. They stand and look out across the still-warm grass at a stand of trees dark-green against the dark-blue sky, lights from distant houses like dull yellow stars.

Afterwards, during class, she thinks about an affair, what it would mean. She tries out the statistician's point of view: what is one small individual event, if the aggregate goes, nevertheless, in its direction? Chalk; blending stump; rag; chalk. Her hand moves smoothly up and down across the nappy surface of the newsprint. Her thoughts move, as seamlessly as in dreams, back and forth between Michael and her easel, exhilarated and afraid.

What is desire?

Early in our marriage we went hiking in November woods out past 495, near Bolton. A place no one knew about.

When we came to the last rock in the creek, the distance between it and the bank was bigger than it had looked from the other side. The bank was steep, an uphill jump, and in the channel between, the water looked unexpectedly deep. I jumped and made it. I fell forward with my palms on the frozen mud. A little early snow lay melting in the chill sun.

"I can't," Faith said. She stood on the wet rock and looked at me. She spread her hands in mock helplessness, palms out. One hand held a stone from the far side of the creek. It lay smooth and wet in her palm, a dark slate-grey, worried into a flattened triangle by the creek's action. Her thumb closed over it. The thumbnail, rimmed with dirt, was bitten into a ragged V.

"Come on," I said. "Just jump."

"I can't. I'll fall."

Between us the brown creek water rolled over stones and broken branches and slick mossy mud. Its depths held dense ochre shadows. I planted one foot at the edge of the bank and stretched my legs until my other foot found the rock where she stood. My knees locked, anticipating. I held out my hand.

"I'll catch you."

In midjump I held her in both arms above the narrow rushing water. She was trembling lightly, her body warm through her padded cotton coat. I put my face against her bare neck. The skin smelled of onions.

The drawer resisted me at first. Then it gave so abruptly I was thrown back against the side of the bed. I began lifting out cotton underpants and slips and flannel pajamas. They were neatly folded and smelled of laundry soap, a nunlike fragrance of cool hands and downcast eyes. Under pajamas printed with yellow roses I found the book. *Figure Drawing Made Easy*, by Michael Otto Basker. I turned it over. On the back of the dust jacket was the author's photograph. Light from the small round lamp on the dresser illuminated the mild eyes, the shallow dimple at the left-hand corner of the mouth, the beginning of a smile.

I imagined Faith looking up Basker's name in the card catalogue, finding this book, going every day to the 709s to look at the photograph. One afternoon, with the bells in University Chapel tolling five o'clock, she steals the book. Peeling away the security label, she pushes the book to the bottom of her green leather purse, and its catch snaps shut.

I slipped the book back under the same pair of flowered pajamas. When I put the other things back on top, something fell out, bounced once on the rug, and rolled under the dresser. I reached under and picked it up—a small, flat, nearly triangular rock, blue-grey now that it was dry. It sat in my palm, powdery and cool. I put it back between folds of flannel and closed the drawer.

Faith was late getting home from class. I stood at the front window until I saw the Toyota. Our street with its carved and garlanded wooden houses was nearly all dark. By the time she came in, I was sitting in the greenish light from the television watching a rerun of the NBA Finals.

"I don't know," Faith said. She stood in the middle of the living room. "Maybe I should drop this class. There was a bad accident on 128, right before I-90. An ambulance—two ambulances. And I don't know how many police cars. There was glass all over my side of the road."

"128's pretty safe, actually," I said. "And if there's just been an accident, then the odds are in your favor."

That isn't true, of course. As practically everyone knows (but hardly anyone believes), you can have a coin land heads up nine times in a row, and the tenth time you toss it, the odds are still fifty-fifty it will come up heads.

Faith, who is completely unable to think in percentages, which she claims is like having a mind full of hedgehogs, said, "When your number's up, it's up."

"I've explained this to you before, Faith." Exasperation crept into my voice, and I stopped to smooth it out. "Statistics predict for the aggregate but not for the individual." Now I sounded like a textbook, but at least it was the truth. "The individual can still choose, even though the general outcome is predetermined. There's no call to be fatalistic."

"Well, what do you think I should do?" She ran her hands through her thick hair and rubbed her eyes. Her fingers came away with blue smudges on them.

"You could take the back roads, if you're worried."

I let my eyes move back to the TV screen, where Magic Johnson was poised for a foul shot. He missed. After a couple of minutes, Faith went upstairs. I heard the dresser drawer groan. Then the bedroom door clicked shut.

They stand on the lawn out of sight of the studio in the warm rainy night. When they kiss, he pulls her off balance, so that she has to stand on the balls of her feet to keep from falling against him. His hand finds the cool wide root of her breast where it spreads out into grainy muscle under her arm.

His dry lips, his mustache feel strange. Her arms come around him, slender back, narrow shoulder blades. His hair, when she combs it slowly with her fingers, feels as she imagined. Ashes, ashes: all fall down.

She didn't expect his body to be so real, as real as Donny's or Joe's. Panic falls on her like a drop cloth.

To predict an event, you have to calculate the probability not just of the most likely path from earlier events but of all possible paths. That's where I went wrong. Yesterday, a Tuesday, Faith was in bed when I got home. The boys were whining and scuffling outside the bedroom door. I sent them down to the kitchen to spoil their dinner with Doritos and Classic Coke. Then I knocked and went in.

"I quit the class," Faith said. "I think I'm coming down with something. There're only two more meetings anyway." She looked up at me. The lines across her forehead deepened, regular and concentric as the striations on a clamshell. Her eyes were lightless.

I fed the boys and bathed them and read to them. When I came to bed, Faith seemed to be asleep. The plate I'd put on her night table, with its toast and tidy pile of scrambled eggs, looked untouched. The venetian blinds were still open. I left them that way and lay down in the stripes of light from the streetlamp.

After half an hour or so, Faith stirred. Up on one elbow, she hesitated. I could feel her watching me. I kept my eyes shut until she slid carefully out of bed. Then I opened them.

At the foot of the bed, she paused. She stood in front of the long mirror over the dresser. Her legs below the short blue cotton night-gown looked too sturdy for its ruffles.

From where I lay, I could see her reflection. In the light from the streetlamps outside, her uncombed hair stuck out around her ears in corkscrews. She raised the nightgown until it was bunched up under her arms. There in the mirror was her body, somehow startling. The flattened breasts with their sloping dark nipples; the line of brown hair striping the belly; the silvery stretch marks along the flanks like watermarks. When she twisted around to look, the same marks shone faintly on the backs of her thighs. I read her face as she looked at herself in the mirror: her eyes asked how she could let a stranger see this body. She let the nightgown fall.

She sat down on the edge of the bed. Gently, slowly, she pulled open the middle drawer of the dresser. The noise made her turn to look at me. I shut my eyes in time. When I opened them, her head was bent. Her back was toward me, but I knew she'd slid the book out from under the soft, washed-out flannel and was holding it be-tween her hands. I knew the image that she saw. I knew the face looking back at her in the dim barred light, the mild eyes like the eyes of the Puritans in anonymous old-fashioned portraits.

Faith had chosen virtue after all: a photograph, an imaginary lover. I should have been glad. But I had wanted to understand. It may be true, as my mother says, that understanding is the booby prize. But when you can't feel things for yourself, can only imagine them, what else is there?

Insomnia began its pinprick scurrying in my head. The bedroom clocks ticked, snipping off precise small quantities of time.

Nothing

They must have been waiting all afternoon for someone like me to come along. Sitting in the narrow lane between a low bungalow with a green-painted porch and Bethel Baptist Church. Hot; at loose ends under that loud sky. Three of them had their backs against the stone wall of the church, legs in cutoff jeans stretched out in front of them, while the fourth, a few feet away, drew pictures in the cindery dust. The back of his undershirt, cropped raggedly just above his waist, showed a large grey patch of sweat. He kept his head bent close to the ground and drew with his index finger. The watchers snickered. The artist wet his finger again, leaving a thin crust of dirt on his lower lip. He added a few more strokes. He smiled down at the ground, then up into the painfully blue sky.

The sun shone straight down into the alley. They all grinned and punched each other and one of them pulled a joint out of his jeans pocket. They squatted in the dirt, sucking fiercely when the joint came to them and squinting past each other. The forward set of their shoulders said, Men's Business.

That was when I came along, driving slowly back from the doctor's with my sad news. Big silver Volvo waiting for the light to change. Must have a/c, all them windows up. Silly bitch can't see the fuckin light's busted.

One minute I was studying the little church, following its squat lines and thinking, as I always did when I passed it, about the people who'd built it—what they dreamed about and who they loved and how they punished their children. The next minute I was thrown sideways. My shoulder hit the side of the door; then I bounced the other way. The stick shift banged my knee.

Two on the right side, two on the left, they rocked the car back and forth, side to side. They moved with the absorbed, purposeful elegance of dancers. Absurdly, there came to my mind for an instant the face of the first boy I ever dated, so intent on me that once he walked right through my screen door. The muscles stood out in their shoulders and upper arms, dark skin almost purple. On their faces was the ferocious tenderness of a mother who rocks her squalling baby.

I never drove in the city without locking the doors. They couldn't get in; but I couldn't get out. I couldn't put the car in gear and drive forward. What if I ran over them, parts of them? I was caught. What if, as Daniel and I had so hoped, I *had* been pregnant? I know the uterus curves around the fetus like a hand holding an apple; but I could see it, little shrimp fetus—little imaginary child—brutally sloshing, rocking as I was rocking in the belly of the Volvo. The air in front of me filled with little black dots, like the veil on a hat. I felt for the seat-belt buckle, couldn't find it. I leaned to my right and put my head down.

The rocking stopped. When I sat up, there was a face in the side window, surprisingly young, a child's face almost: nose splayed against the glass, five pads of fingers pressing on either side. His eyes were two or three inches from my face. A child's eyes. I rocked on the edge of them. Brown; no, blue; no, brown and blue. I pulled my eyes away.

I saw my chance then. The group's fine, feverish concentration had broken. The three other boys had moved around in front of the car and they were dancing. They jerked and jumped and banged on the fenders. As if it belonged to someone else, I watched my foot find the clutch. My hand grabbed the gearshift and shoved it into reverse.

The car shot away, scattering boys in its wake. Naked arms and legs seemed to fly out from their bodies. I punched the switch, and all the windows in the car came down with a soft collective thud. The block blurred past in one long, hot breath—stone church the color of dried blood, spindly leaning porches, catalpa trees with yellowed leaves limp as old newspapers. At the Dairy Mart on the corner, with its plate glass held together by a huge spidery asterisk of masking tape, I backed left. I took the long way home.

When Daniel looked up from stirring the chicken curry to ask what had happened to me, eyes crinkling with concern, I told him, nothing. When he asked what the doctor had found, I told him. Nothing.

That night I dreamed of it, the rocking, the face flat against the glass. I woke with a wordless shout. Warm, wet air clung to my bare arms and legs. I could hear the sound of crickets through the open windows. Above us the skylight was empty, a square of grey-washed darkness; the moon had drifted out of it like a boat untied.

Kath? What is it? Daniel half-whispered.

I had a dream.

What about?

No, I said. In the dense heat wrapping us, I shivered.

Daniel's hand in my damp hair smelled like coriander. For a second I thought we would make love, we would try again, as we had so often; but he only began to untangle the long cord of his radio ear-plug, which had wrapped itself around my shoulder.

Do you want anything?

No, I whispered. Nothing.

He fitted the plug into his ear.

They had been bronze, those child-eyes, the color of muddy water in sunlight. Close up, the ragged rim of blue around the pupil was like the spark when you touch hands with someone on a cold day— that small soft explosion of surprise.

The
Cost
of
Anything

It is a funeral without a body. An oxymoron, my
father would have said, leaning back and talking past his cigarette so
that smoke ribboned out around it and dwindled to lavender above his
head. My mother, kneeling beside me in her long-sleeved black dress,
elbows tucked in at her sides, has done what my father wanted. With
secret relief—cremation is neater than burial—she has followed exactly the instructions in my father's Living Will.

She turns to look at me. Behind the netting of her black veil, her
face is as composed as always; as always, it makes me want to fidget,
hum, do something unruly, as if I were nine instead of nineteen. Her
dark eyes, legacy of her Russian mother, burn without light: icon

eyes. I think: She doesn't care that he's dead. At a funeral without a body, would there be mourners without grief?

"Sophie," she whispers, barely moving her lips. But I don't know what she wants.

I turn back to the altar, but I can't concentrate. Last night I lay in my single bed, my girl's bed, sleepless; now I am tired. Underneath, piled up in my bones, is the deeper accumulated weariness of waiting for my father to die, the weekly trips upstate from teachers' college to find him smaller each time, cancer securing the lush red sponges of his lungs until they branched hard and white like coral.

The altar boys finish lighting the candles, six tall ones spiking up through the massed white flowers on the altar, answering the squat votive candles below. What would I pray for, kneeling at the altar rail with my wooden match suspended over the red glass cup, its flame searing my fingers? Isn't it always the impossible we ask for, in the moment when the wick catches? Smoke fills my throat and I can feel a rumble deeper down, the beginning of asthma. I won't give in to it now, not now. Daddy in the dark holding my hand between his large cool ones while we wait for the pills to work. I lie in bed propped on an inverted wooden chair, terrified by the insect noise in my chest, and he cups his hands over my ears as if that would shut it out.

I pull myself back to *here, now*, this church, this pew, this hard rubber-coated kneeler. More flowers are banked along the altar rail and up the steps to the sanctuary. White, all white: spiny chrysanthemums, peonies, gladioli like medieval weapons. Behind me I can feel the weight of all the people who have come, their faces massed together like the flowers. I realize I'm waiting for my father to emerge from their midst and drop into the empty space beside me, shaking snow off his overcoat, leaning his forearms on the cold yellow wood of the pew. Late for Mass, out parking the car.

Maybe I really am fidgeting, because my mother whispers, "Sophie. *Sonya.*" The nickname means she's displeased. When I was little, the more diminutive the name, the more serious the crime, all the way down to the smallest, tiny *Sonyechka*, usually accompanied by a slap. I'd be sent to bed without dinner then. Later my father would come upstairs to say goodnight with a Lebanon bologna sandwich flattened in his pocket. The dream thieves come on an empty stomach, he'd say. Eat, Sophie, so you don't miss any dreams.

Looking straight ahead, I try to see my father's face; but I can't.

Above the altar hangs a huge crucifix with a figure on it the size of a four-year-old child. Its head is tucked to one side, its arms and legs impossibly twisted, as if the bones inside them had gone soft. The long curled fingers seem to cup the metal spikes. The feet have slender tendons and hard yellow toenails, like my father's naked feet protruding from the white hospital sheet. Unbearable that they should be seen by strangers; I pulled the stiff sheet over them, and the blanket woven in little squares like a waffle. He thanked me with his eyelids—his throat swarmed with pus and he couldn't speak any more. Around us was the blank hospital smell.

If only Father Sawyers would finish, standing with his arms along the sides of the lectern, leaning confidentially forward. His chest in black silk bulges over the top of the lectern; a sculpted puff of hair sits on his head like a cake. I can't hear what he's saying, as if his words were pitched too high for my ears, like those whistles only dogs can hear. Instead, my head is suddenly full of a poem my Uncle Ilya likes to recite.

> Little Willy in the best of sashes
> Fell in the fire and was burned to ashes;
> Now even though the room grows chilly,
> No one cares to poke up Willy.

Horribly apt, it refuses to go away. I hear it playing over and over in my head. At last Father Sawyers mounts the steps to the altar and stands for a moment with his back to us in the black beetle shell of his vestments. Then he turns and makes the Sign of the Cross.

My mother and I go up the aisle first, as if at wedding, and pew by pew the guests fall in behind us. But something is missing. Music, there's no music. No "Onward, Christian Soldiers," no "Dies Irae," nothing but the sandpaper shuffling of heavy winter boots. My father's funeral instructions didn't say no music. I look sideways at my mother, who is walking with her head up, shoulders back, no slimy tracks of tears across her cheeks. Feeling my eyes on her, she reaches into her coat pocket and hands me a clean white handkerchief ironed into a square. My nose is running. Hating her, I take it.

At the back of the church we become a kind of receiving line: one by one people slide past, seizing our hands and murmuring. "Minna, Sophie, Minna, Sophie," an incantation punctuated now and then by "Robert"—roll call of the living and the dead. My mother nods, bows faintly from the waist, pays out a thin smile. Except for her mouth, her flat, Slavic face is motionless, impassive as a melon. No grief in it; no passion of any kind.

Hands grasp mine and slip away. My mother's damp handkerchief is balled tight in my left hand and I keep my right hand stretched out. Minna, Sophie; Minna, Sophie, Robert. *Little Willy.* The aunts, my father's two much older sisters, fur collars drawn up around their faces like ruffs; Uncle Ilya, who lays his leather-gloved hand against the back of my neck under my hair and holds me like that for a moment with his queer light eyes that aren't at all like Mother's. "Sonyechka," he says, breathing vodka at me; and then he's gone.

The rest of the faces—my parents' few friends, my father's co-workers from the Still River Post Office, the other secretaries where my mother works—run together, passing through our brief two-woman gauntlet. My mother and I touch them, one by one; we do not touch each other.

This is the house I was born in. In pregnancy my mother became more and more melancholy and Slavic and in the end refused to go to any of the hospitals in Scranton; everyone knew that in hospitals you could die. Instead, the doctor came out to Still River and I was born upstairs in her wide wooden bed. The house is two hundred years old, more or less. Added onto here and there over the years, it shambles along a rocky shelf, a glacial deposit starred with pine and spruce that ends abruptly at a well of denser forest.

In the kitchen Marie lies stretched along the bottom of the refrigerator where the warm air comes out. She lifts her head and looks at me out of skeptical yellow eyes, all black, a midnight cat. "Yes, and I'm Marie of Rumania," my mother would say whenever my father, waving his arms around the kitchen, launched into one of his lectures on the meaning of history; and his hands would fall to his sides and hang still. My father named her, but she is my mother's cat, composed, indifferent.

I open the refrigerator door. Inside are mostly things in bottles— ketchup, mustard, mayonnaise, the kind of thing you never throw out. There's a carton of milk on the top shelf, and a six-pack of yogurt in different flavors.

"I don't see why you had to wear your rubber coat," says my mother, coming into the kitchen. She sits down on the old cretonne-covered sofa in front of the wood-stove and pulls off her black high-heeled shoes. She aligns them carefully on the rag rug. Marie leaps onto the back of the sofa. Turning once on the narrow ledge, she lies down across the back of my mother's neck like a furpiece.

"It's a down coat, Mother." The expiration date on the carton of milk is nine days ago.

"Yellow. Does yellow show respect for the dead, Sonya? I ask you."

"I don't think Daddy would have minded," I say. My head is inside the refrigerator.

"What?"

I say, loud this time, "I'm not a child anymore." I use a cherished expression of my father's. "I wish you'd quit giving me grief about the way I dress."

"Grief," my mother says, in a tone that's almost thoughtful. And then, "You think being in college makes you grown? Just like your father. Everything out of books."

I turn around. She is sitting with one stockinged foot in her hands, rubbing the arch with her thumb. In the evenings after supper my father liked to open the door of the wood-stove so that firelight shone across the wide planked floor, and the two of us would sit on the sofa eating Hershey bars and oranges.

I take an ice cube in my hand and squeeze it, make the cold go deep, squeeze it till it burns. "You don't understand," I say. "Just like you never understood—"

The word I don't say hangs in the air between us. *Him*. My mother stiffens and reaches up to smooth her hair. Her eyes are almost black. She says, "It's past three. I have things to see to." She gets up and goes to the doorway, still wearing Marie, two paws bunched in each hand to keep her in place. On the threshold she turns.

"Grief," she says. "Grief. You don't even know what it is."

She goes into the living room. I let the refrigerator door thud shut. I toss the ice overhand into the sink, where it clatters on the porcelain, and wipe my hands on the blue dishtowel threaded through the door handle.

I move down the hall with the soft step of an intruder. The Elbow, I used to call it, its shape dictated by the curve of the bluff. At the crook, just before the passage turns and opens into my father's study, I stop. In the other rooms it was no different from the way it used to be, with Daddy at the back of the house, "working." This room will be truly empty.

Stumbling on the shallow step leading down to it, I almost fall into the room. The smell of tobacco, the big oak desk with its drift of papers, the blue-painted wooden swivel chair half-turned. But the room is gelid and dark.

I push up the thermostat as far as it will go, eighty, eight-five, ninety, and snap on the old metal gooseneck lamp that sits on the desk. Deep colors spring out from the bookshelves. On the floor are two small Navaho rugs in the same rose and dark blue and ruby. The corner of one is flipped back. I crouch down to straighten it.

He loved history: the Greeks, the Romans, the Civil War—it didn't matter. He was in love with history. People think the past is sealed off, unreachable, as if yesterday were a landslide between us and everything that went before. My father saw it differently. "People remake the past every day of their lives," he'd say. "Trade one version for another. Something that makes sense, helps them get by." Historians, he thought, were storytellers, not reporters.

In the doors of the tall mahogany wardrobe that belonged to my father's grandmother are two long, narrow mirrors. Slanted in some odd way, they copy me twice: two wavery, long-necked girls in black wool suits too big for them. The Calvinist Witch, my mother calls my great-grandmother Alyssa, who raised my father. She died before I was born; but I grew up hating her, the woman who used to lock my father in this very wardrobe. When I was small, I was afraid to be alone with it, afraid the mirrored doors would open and her skinny freckled hand would reach out and pull me in.

Metal filing cabinets, a rickety typing table, an old padded easy chair. There is even a tiny refrigerator in the corner, the kind you see in motel rooms. Over the years my father made the room self-sufficient, filling it with more and more things and spending more and more time there, like a garden snail pulling deeper into the humid cave of its shell.

On the wall above the desk is a large square of dark-brown corkboard where my father pinned notes to himself, clippings, sayings he liked. I wrote to him every week after I left for college, separate letters just to him. He'd send back clippings. Items from the *Scranton Times*, quotations from books he was reading, magazine articles that had something to do with my courses. Attached to them would be a note, a single sentence: *Thought you might like to see this. Love, Robert.* I suppose each clipping spent some time up on the corkboard first. Now it holds only a typed quotation with *Thoreau* written in blue ink underneath: "The cost of a thing is the amount of what I will call life which is required to be exchanged for it, immediately or in the long run."

On the desk is the metronome I broke when I was nine, ending the argument over piano lessons. Picking it up, I blow off the dust. One corner is gone, and the broken-off pendulum pricks my thumb, leaving a tiny bright bubble of blood. My father's navy-blue beret is looped over one arm of the wooden swivel chair. He said he wore it so that no one would ask him for directions; I knew it was to make him look like a scholar and not a mailman. I pick it up and hold it in both hands. The wool smells of smoke and Dial soap. I can see the beret slanted across his thinning hair, and the turned-up collar of his red down jacket; but I can't see the face in between.

We stood on the rocky outcropping just beyond the end of the house, the two of us ankle-deep in new snow. That morning he and my mother and I had sat in a row on one side of the baronial desk with the well-known Philadelphia oncologist on the other. Behind his head hung a bland arrangement of diplomas in dark frames. He'd coughed and said without looking at us, Less than a year.

Bells of snow hung in the pine branches. My father held the pipe he'd switched to too late, his knuckles shiny purple in the cold. The bowl, which had a face carved into it, was shaped into a head with the top sliced off, like a boiled egg. When he sucked in, the match caught. Sparks flew out of the ebony forehead and shot up into the dusk.

"Daddy," I said. He was silent. We stood listening to the creak of chickadees at the feeder.

"Daddy."

He held up his hand. "Look." Beyond the jut of rock we stood on, where the land dropped away, two squirrels were chasing each other through dense young pines, leaping from one to the next. Behind them a trail of empty boughs, wagging, flung down clots of snow.

"Dad."

" 'Small rooms or dwellings set the mind in the right path,' " said my father. " 'Large ones cause it to go astray.' Leonardo da Vinci."

I gave up then. I reached up and kissed him on the mouth. Below the sharpness of his moustache, his lower lip was soft and cold. The last of the light had gone. Behind his head, the eastern sky had darkened to the color of his beret. There were no stars. We stood in silence on the snowy ledge while the last birds made their bleak, interrogative sounds.

My father swallowed and his throat moved. The smoke from his pipe sifted between us. "We should go in. Your mother will have supper ready."

The beret feels rough between my hands. It's odd. Why is the smell of smoke trapped in the wool not stale, but spicy and sharp? As sharp as it was that evening a year ago. Across the room a window looks out over the bluff where we stood then. As if by moving closer I could get back inside that time, I walk over to it. Below me, distorted by the old wavy glass, a small fire burns in the darkening air. A figure moves up to it and jumps away, up and away, over and over. I lean my forehead against the dirty glass. Absurdly, I think of Rumpelstiltskin in front of his cooking fire: *Today I brew, tomorrow I'll bake; then the*—something—*child I'll take.*

I throw the beret onto the desk and run, along the Elbow, across the kitchen, into the living room and out through the French doors. Cold snowy air fills my nose and mouth. As I round the corner of the house, my mother, black coat flapping, flings something into the fire. She grabs a rake from the ground and thrusts it into the flames, lunging and stabbing. "Fool," she puffs out. "*Durak!*"

"Mother!" I shout.

Her head jerks up. The light from the fire between us throws her eyes into shadow and strikes off the bones of her face. Her hair snakes wildly around her head. Behind her, above the well of dense pine and spruce, the sunset sky is a deep rose. She stands still, her shoulders hunched forward, her hand on the rake handle shaking.

"You'll be cold, Sophie. Without your coat," she says in a businesslike voice. Then she shudders.

"Mother, what are you doing?" Coming closer, I skid on the slick crust of frozen leaves and pine needles.

"Cleaning up," says my mother. She leans on her rake. Soot shines on her cheeks and her hair is powdered with ash. "You can *see* that." With the back of one hand, she pushes at her damp hair, leaves a black streak across her forehead.

On the ground are several large, leather-covered albums, open, their pages torn out. The fire buzzes and snaps around the half-burned photographs. Uncle Ilya, his head thrown back, laughing. Great-grandmother Alyssa as a girl, with pale ratted hair and a high lace collar. Flames lick her silk-covered bosom. As her photograph curls and crumbles, it uncovers another: my mother in a round hat of gleaming plaited straw with a plume on one side. Behind her are the metal steps of an airplane; propeller blades slice across a corner of the picture. She kneels beside a little girl in a coat too big for her and a cloth bonnet that throws a triangle of shadow. Standing there with the heat of my mother's fire in my face, I can feel that coat again, dense blue-grey wool solid as clay.

They're all there on the rocky ledge with us, the people I used to look at for hours, holding the fat slippery albums too big for my lap, the heavy pages thudding as I turned them. "What are you doing," I shout. "Will you *stop*?"

"They're stories," my mother says, staring down at the photographs. "That's all they are. They're not what really happened." She goes back to her raking, harvesting ashes and bits of charred wood, pushing black clods of paper back and forth. A new batch of photographs is swept forward, the rake fanning them out across a momentary lull in the flames; and there is my father's face.

The pale hair, already beginning to recede, sweeps back from his wide forehead. Bare-chested, in baggy flowered bathing trunks, he has one arm around my mother, who wears a light-colored sarong and a hibiscus tucked behind one ear. They are on their honeymoon, a week on Oahu, which my father won by completing a limerick for a soap advertisement on WBLJ. "The best aid to beauty, bar none." My father is squinting into the camera and sweating. The edges of the photograph curl in blackened points like the petals of the flower in my mother's hair.

Without thinking, I crouch down and reach into the fire. It sears my hand. I jump back, trip over the albums and send them skittering across the icy ground. I stumble to the other side of the fire. I put my hands on my mother's shoulders and shake her and shake her.

"What are you doing? What are you *doing*?"

Her eyes are as blank as if she were snowblind. "He had no right," she shouts into my face. She is trembling. "Can't you understand, Sophie? No right."

She looks up at me, and I do not want to understand, but I do. She can see that. She slumps. Under my hands her shoulders are bone-thin. I am all that's holding her up.

She says, just above a whisper, "We'll never catch him now."

Her nose is running. She wipes her hand across her glistening upper lip. I let go of her shoulders and push her hair behind her ears, first one, then the other. "Mama."

The fire burns down, and the smoke thins to a single narrow stream. The air is still and cold. Everything has crystal edges and catches the light; sounds are thin and pure, like the current of air through a flute. We can hear ice crackling in the pines overhead. Their branches cross and snap in the little light wind, tapping out uninterpretable messages. We stand watching the fire crawl across the last of the album pages, watching the photographs soften and yield.

Other Iowa Short Fiction Award and John Simmons Short Fiction Award Winners

1992
My Body to You, Elizabeth Searle
Judge: James Salter

1992
Imaginary Men, Enid Shomer
Judge: James Salter

1991
The Ant Generator,
Elizabeth Harris
Judge: Marilynne Robinson

1991
Traps, Sondra Spatt Olsen
Judge: Marilynne Robinson

1990
A Hole in the Language,
Marly Swick
Judge: Jayne Anne Phillips

1989
Lent: The Slow Fast,
Starkey Flythe, Jr.
Judge: Gail Godwin

1989
Line of Fall, Miles Wilson
Judge: Gail Godwin

1988
The Long White,
Sharon Dilworth
Judge: Robert Stone

1988
The Venus Tree, Michael Pritchett
Judge: Robert Stone

1987
Fruit of the Month, Abby Frucht
Judge: Alison Lurie

1987
Star Game, Lucia Nevai
Judge: Alison Lurie

1986
Eminent Domain, Dan O'Brien
Judge: Iowa Writers' Workshop

1986
Resurrectionists, Russell Working
Judge: Tobias Wolff

1985
Dancing in the Movies,
Robert Boswell
Judge: Tim O'Brien

1984
Old Wives' Tales, Susan M. Dodd
Judge: Frederick Busch

1983
Heart Failure, Ivy Goodman
Judge: Alice Adams

1982
Shiny Objects, Dianne Benedict
Judge: Raymond Carver

1981
The Phototropic Woman,
Annabel Thomas
Judge: Doris Grumbach

1980
Impossible Appetites,
James Fetler
Judge: Francine du Plessix Gray

1979
Fly Away Home, Mary Hedin
Judge: John Gardner

1978
A Nest of Hooks, Lon Otto
Judge: Stanley Elkin

1977
The Women in the Mirror,
Pat Carr
Judge: Leonard Michaels

1976
The Black Velvet Girl,
C. E. Poverman
Judge: Donald Barthelme

1975
Harry Belten and the
Mendelssohn Violin Concerto,
Barry Targan
Judge: George P. Garrett

1974
After the First Death There Is No
Other, Natalie L. M. Petesch
Judge: William H. Gass

1973
The Itinerary of Beggars,
H. E. Francis
Judge: John Hawkes

1972
The Burning and Other Stories,
Jack Cady
Judge: Joyce Carol Oates

1971
Old Morals, Small Continents,
Darker Times,
Philip F. O'Connor
Judge: George P. Elliott

1970
The Beach Umbrella,
Cyrus Colter
Judges: Vance Bourjaily
and Kurt Vonnegut, Jr.